The Mirror of Kong Ho

ISBN: 978-1-64799-951-3

Ernest Bramah

The Mirror of Kong Ho

ISBN: 978-1-64799-951-3

A lively and amusing collection of letters on western living written by Kong Ho, a Chinese gentleman. These addressed to his homeland, refer to the Westerners in London as barbarians and many of the aids to life in our society give Kong Ho endless food for thought. These are things such as the motor car and the piano; unknown in China at this time.

CONTENTS

INTRODUCTION

ESTIMABLE BARBARIAN,—Your opportune suggestion that I should permit the letters, wherein I have described with undeviating fidelity the customs and manner of behaving of your accomplished race, to be set forth in the form of printed leaves for all to behold, is doubtless gracefully-intentioned, and this person will raise no barrier of dissent against it.

In this he is inspired by the benevolent hope that his immature compositions may to one extent become a model and a by-word to those who in turn visit his own land of Fragrant Purity; for with exacting care he has set down no detail that has not come under his direct observation (although it is not to be denied that here or there he may, perchance, have misunderstood an involved allusion or failed to grasp the inner significance of an act), so that Impartiality necessarily sways his brush, and Truth lurks within his inkpot.

In an entirely contrary manner some, who of recent years have gratified us with their magnanimous presence, have returned to their own countries not only with the internal fittings of many of our palaces (which, being for the most part of a replaceable nature, need be only trivially referred to, the incident, indeed, being generally regarded as a most cordial and pressing variety of foreign politeness), but also—in the lack of highly-spiced actuality—with subtly-imagined and truly objectionable instances. These calumnies they have not hesitated to commit to the form of printed books, which, falling into the hands of the ignorant and undiscriminating, may even suggest to their ill-balanced minds a doubt whether we of the Celestial Empire really are the wisest, bravest, purest, and most enlightened people in existence.

As a parting, it only remains to be said that, in order to maintain unimpaired the quaint-sounding brevity and archaic construction of your prepossessing language, I have engraved most of the remarks upon the receptive tablets of my mind as they were uttered. To one who can repeat the Five Classics without stumbling this is a contemptible achievement. Let it be an imposed obligation, therefore, that you retain these portions unchanged as a test and a proof to all who may read. Of my own deficient words, I can only in truest courtesy maintain that any alteration must of necessity make them less offensively commonplace than at present they are.

The Sign and immutable Thumb-mark of, Kong Ho

By a sure hand to the House of one Ernest Bramah.

THE MIRROR OF KONG HO

LETTER I

Concerning the journey. The unlawful demons invoked by certain of the barbarians; their power and the manner of their suppression. Suppression. The incredible obtuseness of those who attend within tea-houses. The harmonious attitude of a person of commerce.

VENERATED SIRE (at whose virtuous and well-established feet an unworthy son now prostrates himself in spirit repeatedly),—

Having at length reached the summit of my journey, that London of which the merchants from Canton spoke so many strange and incredible things, I now send you filial salutations three times increased, and in accordance with your explicit command I shall write all things to you with an unvarnished brush, well assured that your versatile object in committing me to so questionable an enterprise was, above all, to learn the truth of these matters in an undeviating and yet open-headed spirit of accuracy and toleration.

Of the perils incurred while travelling in the awe-inspiring devices by which I was transferred from shore to shore and yet further inland, of the utter absence of all leisurely dignity on the part of those controlling their movements, and of the almost unnatural self-opinionatedness which led them to persist in starting at a stated and prearranged time, even when this person had courteously pointed out to them by irrefutable omens that neither the day nor the hour was suitable for the venture, I have already written. It is enough to assert that a similar want of prudence was maintained on

1

every occasion, and, as a result, when actually within sight of the walls of this city, we were involved for upwards of an hour in a very evilly-arranged yellow darkness, which, had we but delayed for a day, as I strenuously advised those in authority after consulting the Sacred Flat and Round Sticks, we should certainly have avoided.

Concerning the real nature of the devices by which the ships are propelled at sea and the carriages on land, I must still unroll a blank mind until I can secretly, and without undue hazard, examine them more closely. If, as you maintain, it is the work of captive demons hidden away among their most inside parts, it must be admitted that these usually intractable beings are admirably trained and controlled, and I am wide-headed enough to think that in this respect we might—not-withstanding our nine thousand years of civilised refinement—learn something of the methods of these barbarians. The secret, however, is jealously guarded, and they deny the existence of any supernatural forces; but their protests may be ignored, for there is undoubtedly a powerful demon used in a similar way by some of the boldest of them, although its employment is unlawful. A certain kind of chariot is used for the occupation of this demon, and those who wish to invoke it conceal their faces within masks of terrifying design, and cover their hands and bodies with specially prepared garments, without which it would be fatal to encounter these very powerful spirits. While yet among the habitations of men, and in crowded places, they are constrained to use less powerful demons, which are lawful, but when they reach the unfrequented paths they throw aside all restraint, and, calling to their aid the forbidden spirit (which they do by secret movements of the hands), they are carried forward by its agency at a speed unattainable by merely human means. By day the demon looks forth from three white eyes, which at night have a penetrating brilliance equal to the fiercest glances of the Sacred Dragon in anger. If any person incautiously stands in its way it utters a warning cry of intolerable rage, and should the presumptuous one neglect to escape to the roadside and there prostrate himself reverentially before it, it seizes him by the body part and contemptuously hurls him bruised and unrecognisable into the boundless space of the around. Frequently the demon causes the chariot to rise into the air, and it is credibly asserted by discriminating witnesses (although this person only sets down as incapable of denial that which he has actually beheld) that some have maintained an unceasing flight through the middle air for a distance of many li. Occasionally the captive demon escapes from the bondage of those who have invoked it, through some incautious

2

gesture or heretical remark on their part, and then it never fails to use them grievously, casting them to the ground wounded, consuming the chariot with fire, and passing away in the midst of an exceedingly debased odour, by which it is always accompanied after the manner of our own earth spirits.

This being, as this person has already set forth, an unlawful demon on account of its power when once called up, and the admitted uncertainty of its movements, those in authority maintain a stern and inexorable face towards the practice. To entrap the unwary certain persons (chosen on account of their massive outlines, and further protected from evil influences by their pure and consistent habits) keep an unceasing watch. When one of them, himself lying concealed, detects the approach of such a being, he closely observes the position of the sun, and signals to the other a message of warning. Then the second one, shielded by the sanctity of his life and rendered inviolable by the nature of his garments—his sandals alone being capable of overturning any demon from his path should it encounter them—boldly steps forth into the road and holds out before him certain sacred emblems. So powerful are these that at the sight the unlawful demon confesses itself vanquished, and although its whole body trembles with ill-contained rage, and the air around is poisoned by its discreditable exhalation, it is devoid of further resistance. Those in the chariot are thereupon commanded to dismiss it, and being bound in chains they are led into the presence of certain lesser mandarins who administer justice from a raised dais.

"Behold!" exclaims the chief of the captors, when the prisoners have been placed in obsequious attitudes before the lesser mandarins, "thus the matter chanced: The honourable Wang, although disguised under the semblance of an applewoman, had discreetly concealed himself by the roadside, all but his head being underneath a stream of stagnant water, when, at the eighth hour of the morning, he beheld these repulsive outcasts approaching in their chariot, carried forward by the diabolical vigour of the unlawful demon. Although I had stationed myself several li distant from the accomplished Wang, the chariot reached me in less than a breathing space of time, those inside assuming their fiercest and most aggressive attitudes, and as they came repeatedly urging the demon to increased exertions. Their speed exceeded that of the swallow in his hymeneal flight, all shrubs and flowers by the wayside withered incapably at the demon's contaminating glance, running water ceased to flow, and the road itself was scorched at

3

their passage, the earth emitting a dull bluish flame. These facts, and the times and the distances, this person has further inscribed in a book which thus disposes of all possible defence. Therefore, O lesser mandarins, let justice be accomplished heavily and without delay; for, as the proverb truly says, 'The fiercer the flame the more useless the struggles of the victim.'"

At this point the prisoners frequently endeavour to make themselves heard, protesting that in the distance between the concealed Wang and the one who stands accusing them they had thrice stopped to repair their innermost details, had leisurely partaken of food and wine, and had also been overtaken, struck, and delayed by a funeral procession. But so great is the execration in which these persons are held, that although murderers by stealth, outlaws, snatchers from the body, and companies of men who by strategy make a smaller sum of money appear to be larger, can all freely testify their innocence, raisers of this unlawful demon must not do so, and they are beaten on the head with chains until they desist.

Then the lesser mandarins, raising their voices in unison, exclaim, "The amiable Tsay-hi has reported the matter in a discreet and impartial spirit. Hear our pronouncement: These raisers of illegal spirits shall each contribute ten taels of gold, which shall be expended in joss-sticks, in purifying the road which they have scorched, and in alleviating the distress of the poor and virtuous of both sexes. The praiseworthy Tsay-hi, moreover, shall embroider upon his sleeve an honourable sign in remembrance of the event. Let drums now be beat, and our verdict loudly proclaimed throughout the province."

These things, O my illustrious father (although on account of my contemptible deficiencies of style much may seem improbable to your all-knowing mind), these things I write with an unbending brush; for I set down only that which I have myself seen, or read in their own printed records. Doubtless it will occur to one of your preternatural intelligence that our own system of administering justice, whereby the person who can hire the greater number of witnesses is reasonably held to be in the right, although perhaps not absolutely infallible, is in every way more convenient; but, as it is well said, "To the blind, night is as acceptable as day."

Henceforth you will have no hesitation in letting it be known throughout Yuen-ping that these foreign barbarians do possess

4

secret demons, in spite of their denials. Doubtless I shall presently discover others no less powerful.

With honourable distinction this person has at length grasped the essential details of the spoken language here—not sufficiently well, indeed, to make himself understood on most occasions, or even to understand others, but enough to perceive clearly when he fails to become intelligible or when they experience a like difficulty with him. Upon an earlier occasion, before he had made so much progress, being one day left to his own resources, and feeling an internal lack, he entered what appeared to be a tea-shop of reputable demeanour, and, seating himself at one of the little marble tables, he freely pronounced the carefully-learned word "rice" to the attending nymph. To put aside all details of preparation (into which, indeed, this person could not enter) he waved his hand gracefully, at the same time smiling with an expression of tolerant acquiescence, as of one who would say that what was good enough to be cooked and offered by so entrancing a maiden was good enough to be eaten by him. After remaining in unruffled tranquillity for the full portion of an hour, and observing that no other person around had to wait above half that period, this one began to perceive that the enterprise was not likely to terminate in a manner satisfactory to himself; so that, leaving this place with a few well-chosen phrases of intolerable regret in his own tongue, he entered another, and conducted himself in a like fashion.... Towards evening, with an unperturbed exterior, but materially afflicted elsewhere, this person seated himself within the eleventh tea-shop, and, pointing first towards his own constituents of digestion, then at the fire, and lastly in an upward direction, thereby signified to any not of stunted intellect that he had reached such a condition of mind and body that he was ready to consume whatever the ruling deities were willing to allot, whether boiled, baked, roast, or suspended from a skewer. In this resolve nothing would move him, until—after many maidens had approached with outstretched hands and gestures of despair—there presently entered a person wearing the helmet of a warrior and the manner of a high official, who spoke strongly, yet persuasively, of the virtues of immediate movement and a quiet and reposeful bearing.

Assuredly a people who devote so little attention to the study of food, and all matters connected with it, must inevitably remain barbaric, however skilfully they may feign a superficial refinement. It is said, although I do not commit this matter to my own brush, that among them are more books composed on subjects which have

5

no actual existence than on cooking, and, incredible as it may appear, to be exceptionally round-bodied confers no public honour upon the individual. Should a favourable occasion present itself, there are many who do not scruple to jest upon the subject of food, or, what is incalculably more depraved, upon the scarcity of it.

Nevertheless, there are exceptions of a highly distinguished radiance. Among these must be accounted one into whose presence this person was recently led by our polished and harmonious friend Quang-Tsun, the merchant in tea and spices. This versatile person, whose business-name is spoken of as Jones Bob-Jones, is worthy of all benignant respect, and in a really enlightened country would doubtless be raised to a more exalted position than that of a breaker of outsides (an occupation difficult to express adequately in the written language of a country where it is unknown), for his face is like the sun setting in the time of harvest, his waist garment excessive, and the undoubted symmetry of his middle portions honourable in the extreme. So welcome in my eyes, after witnessing an unending stream of concave and attenuated barbarian ghosts, was the sight of these perfections of Jones Bob-Jones, that instead of the formal greeting of this Island—the unmeaning "How do you do it?"—I shook hands cordially with myself, and exclaimed affectionately in our own language, "Illimitable felicities! How is your stomach?"

"Well," replied Jones Bob-Jones, after Quang-Tsun had interpreted this polite salutation to his understanding, "since you mention it, that's just the trouble; but I'm going on pretty well, thanks. I've tried most of the advertised things, and now my doctor has put me practically on a bread-and-water course—clear soup, boiled fish, plain joint, no sweets, a crumb of cheese, and a bare three glasses of Hermitage."

During this amiable remark (of which, as it is somewhat of a technical nature, I was unable to grasp the contained significance until the agreeable Quang-Tsun had subsequently repeated it several times for my retention), I maintained a consistent expression of harmonious agreement and gratified esteem (suitable, I find, for all like occasions), and then, judging from the sympathetic animation of Jones Bob-Jones's countenance, that it had not improbably been connected with food, I discreetly introduced the subject of sea-snails, preserved in the essence of crushed peaches, by courteously inquiring whether he had ever partaken of such a delicacy.

6

"No," replied the liberal-minded person, when—encouraged by the protruding eagerness of his eyes at the mention of the viand—I had further spoken of the refined flavour of the dish, and explained the manner of its preparation. "I can't say that I have, but it sounds uncommonly good—something like turtle, I should imagine. I'll see if they can get it for me at Pimm's."

This filial tribute goes by a trusty hand, in the person of one Ki Nihy, who is shortly committing himself to the protection of his ancestors and the voracity of the unbounded Bitter Waters; and with brightness and gold it will doubtless reach you in the course of twelve or eighteen moons. The superstitious here, this person may describe, when they wish to send messages from one to another, inscribe upon the outer cover a written representation of the one whose habitation they require, and after affixing a small paper talisman, drop it into a hole in the nearest wall, in the hope that it may be ultimately conveyed to the appointed spot, either by the services of the charitably-disposed passer-by, or by the intervention of the beneficent deities.

With a multiplicity of greetings and many abject expressions of a conscious inferiority, and attested by an unvarying thumb-mark.

KONG HO. (Effete branch of a pure and magnanimous trunk.)

To Kong Ah-Paik, reclining beneath the sign of the Lead Tortoise, in a northerly direction beyond the Lotus Beds outside the city of Yuen-ping. The Middle Flowery Kingdom.

LETTER II

Concerning the ill-destined manner of existence of the hound Hercules. The thoughtlessly-expressed desire of the entrancing maiden and its effect upon a person of susceptible refinement. The opportune (as it may yet be described) visit of one Herbert. The behaviour of those around. Reflections.

VENERATED SIRE (whose large right hand is continuously floating in spirit over the image of this person's dutiful submission),—

Doubtless to your all-consuming prescience, it will at once become plain that I have abandoned the place of residence from which I directed my former badly-written and offensively-constructed letter, the house of the sympathetic and resourceful Maidens Blank, where in return for an utterly inadequate sum of money, produced at stated intervals, this very much inferior person was allowed to partake of a delicately-balanced and somewhat unvarying fare in the company of the engaging of both sexes, and afterwards to associate on terms of honourable equality with them in the chief apartment. The reason and manner of this one's departure are in no degree formidable to his refined manner of conducting any enterprise, but arose partly from an insufficient grasp of the more elaborate outlines of a confessedly involved language, and still more from a too excessive impetuousness in carrying out what at the time he believed to be the ambition of one who had come to exercise a melodious influence over his most internal emotions. Well remarked the Sage, "A piece of gold may be tried between the teeth; a written promise to pay may be disposed of at a sacrifice to one more credulous; but what shall be said of the wind, the Hoang Ho, and the way of a woman?"

To contrive a pitfall for this short-sighted person's immature feet, certain malicious spirits had so willed it that the chief and more autumnal of the Maidens Blank (who, nevertheless, wore an excessively flower-like name), had long lavished herself upon the possession of an obtuse and self-assertive hound, which was in the habit of gratifying this inconsiderable person and those who sat

8

around by continually depositing upon their unworthy garments details of its outer surface, and when the weather was more than usually cold, by stretching its graceful and refined body before the fire in such a way as to ensure that no one should suffer from a too acute exposure to the heat. From these causes, and because it was by nature a hound which even on the darkest night could be detected at a more than reasonable distance away, while at all times it did not hesitate to shake itself freely into the various prepared viands, this person (and doubtless others also) regarded it with an emotion very unfavourable towards its prolonged existence; but observing from the first that those who permitted themselves to be deposited upon, and their hands and even their faces to be hound-tongue-defiled with the most externally cheerful spirit of word suppression, invariably received the most desirable of the allotted portions of food, he judged it prudent and conducive to a settled digestion to greet it with favourable terms and actions, and to refer frequently to its well-displayed proportions, and to the agile dexterity which it certainly maintained in breathing into the contents of every dish. Thus the matter may be regarded as being positioned for a space of time.

One evening I returned at the appointed gong-stroke of dinner, and was beginning, according to my custom, to greet the hound with ingratiating politeness, when the one of chief authority held up a reproving hand, at the same time exclaiming:

"No, Mr. Kong, you must not encourage Hercules with your amiable condescension, for just now he is in very bad odour with us all."

"Undoubtedly," replied this person, somewhat puzzled, nevertheless, that the imperfection should thus be referred to openly by one who hitherto had not hesitated to caress the hound with most intimate details, "undoubtedly the surrounding has a highly concentrated acuteness to-night, but the ever-present characteristic of the hound Hercules is by no means new, for whenever he is in the room—"

At this point it is necessary to explain that the ceremonial etiquette of these barbarian outcasts is both conflicting and involved. Upon most of the ordinary occasions of life to obtrude oneself within the conversation of another is a thing not to be done, yet repeatedly when this unpretentious person has been relating his experience or inquiring into the nature and meaning of certain matters which he has witnessed, he has become aware that his words have been obliterated, as it were, and his remarks diverted from their original

9

intention by the sudden and unanticipated desire of those present to express themselves loudly on some topic of not really engrossing interest. Not infrequently on such occasions every one present has spoken at once with concentrated anxiety upon the condition of the weather, the atmosphere of the room, the hour of the day, or some like detail of contemptible inferiority. At other times maidens of unquestionable politeness have sounded instruments of brass or stringed woods with unceasing vigour, have cast down ornaments of china, or even stood upon each other's—or this person's—feet with assumed inelegance. When, therefore, in the midst of my agreeable remark on the asserted no fragrance of the hound Hercules, a gentleman of habitual refinement struck me somewhat heavily on the back of the head with a reclining seat which he was conveying across the room for the acceptance of a lady, and immediately overwhelmed me with apologies of almost unnecessary profusion, my mind at once leapt to an inspired conclusion, and smiling acquiescently I bowed several times to each person to convey to them an admission of the undoubted fact that to the wise a timely omen before the storm is as effective as a thunderbolt afterwards.

It chanced that there was present the exceptionally prepossessing maiden to whom this person has already referred. So varied and ornate were her attractions that it would be incompetent in one of my less than average ability to attempt an adequate portrayal. She had a light-coloured name with the letters so harmoniously convoluted as to be quite beyond my inferior power of pronunciation, so that if I wished to refer to her in her absence I had to indicate the one I meant by likening her to a full-blown chrysanthemum, a piece of rare jade, an ivory pagoda of unapproachable antiquity, or some other object of admitted grace. Even this description may scarcely convey to you the real extent of her elegant personality; but in her presence my internal organs never failed to vibrate with a most entrancing uncertainty, and even now, at the recollection of her virtuous demeanour, I am by no means settled within myself.

"Well," exclaimed this melodious vision, with sympathetic tact, "if every one is going to disown poor Hercules because he has eaten all our dinners, I shall be quite willing to have him, for he is a dzear ole loveykins, wasn't ums?" (This, O my immaculate and dignified sire, which I transcribe with faithful undeviation, appears to be the dialect of a remote province, spoken only by maidens—both young and of autumnal solitude—under occasional mental stress; as of a native of Shan-si relapsing without consciousness into his uncouth

10

tongue after passing a lifetime in the Capital.) "Don't you think so too, Mr. Kong?"

"When the sun shines the shadow falls, for truly it is said, 'To the faithful one even the voice of the corncrake at evening speaks of his absent love,'" replied this person, so engagingly disconcerted at being thus openly addressed by the maiden that he retained no delicate impression of what she said, or even of what he was replying, beyond an unassuming hope that the nature of his feelings might perchance be inoffensively revealed to her in the semblance of a discreet allegory.

"Perhaps," interposed a person of neglected refinement, turning towards the maiden, "you would like to have a corncrake also, to remind you of Mr. Kong?"

"I do not know what a corncrake is like," replied the maiden with commendable dignity. "I do not think so, however, for I once had a pair of canaries, and I found them very unsatisfying, insipid creatures. But I should love to have a little dog I am sure, only Miss Blank won't hear of it."

"Kong Ho," thought this person inwardly, "not in vain have you burnt joss sticks unceasingly, for the enchanting one has said into your eyes that she would love to partake of a little dog. Assuredly we have recently consumed the cold portion of sheep on more occasions than a strict honourableness could require of those who pay a stated sum at regular intervals, and the change would be a welcome one. As she truly says, the flavour even of canaries is trivial and insignificant by comparison." During the period of dinner— which consisted of eggs and green herbs of the field—this person allowed the contemplation to grow within him, and inspired by a most pleasant and disinterested ambition to carry out the expressed wishes of the one who had spoken, he determined that the matter should be unobtrusively arranged despite the mercenary opposition of the Maidens Blank.

This person had already learned by experience that dogs are rarely if ever exposed for sale in the stalls of the meat venders, the reason doubtless being that they are articles of excessive luxury and reserved by law for the rich and powerful. Those kept by private persons are generally closely guarded when they approach a desirable condition of body, and the hound Hercules would not prove an attractive dish to those who had known him in life. Nevertheless, it is well said, "The Great Wall is unsurmountable, but

11

there are many gaps through," and that same evening I was able to carry the first part of my well-intentioned surprise into effect.

The matter now involves one named Herbert, who having exchanged gifts of betrothal with a maiden staying at the house, was in the habit of presenting himself openly, when he was permitted to see her, after the manner of these barbarians. (Yet even of them the more discriminating acknowledge that our customs are immeasurably superior; for when I explained to the aged father of the Maidens Blank that among us the marriage rites are irrevocably performed before the bride is seen unveiled by man, he sighed heavily and exclaimed that the parents of this country had much to learn.)

The genial-minded Herbert had already acquired for himself the reputation of being one who ceaselessly removes the gravity of others, both by word and action, and from the first he selected this obscure person for his charitable purpose to a most flattering extent. Not only did he—on the pretext that his memory was rebellious—invariably greet me as "Mr. Hong Kong," but on more than one occasion he insisted, with mirth-provoking reference to certain details of my unbecoming garments, that I must surely have become confused and sent a Mrs. Hong Kong instead of myself, and frequently he undermined the gravity of all most successfully by pulling me backwards suddenly by the pigtail, with the plea that he imagined he was picking up his riding-whip. This attractive person was always accompanied by a formidable dog—of convex limbs, shrunken lip, and suspicious demeanour—which he called Influenza, to the excessive amusement of those to whom he related its characteristics. For some inexplicable reason from the first it regarded my lower apparel as being unsuitable for the ordinary occasions of life, and in spite of the low hissing call by which its master endeavoured to attract its attention to himself, it devoted its energies unceasingly to the self-imposed task of removing them fragment by fragment. Nevertheless it was a dog of favourable size and condition, and it need not therefore be a matter for surprise that when the intellectual person Herbert took his departure on the day in question it had to be assumed that it had already preceded him. Having accomplished so much, this person found little difficulty in preparing it tastefully in his own apartment, and making the substitution on the following day.

Although his mind was confessedly enlarged at the success of his venture, and his hopes most ornamentally coloured at the thought

12

of the adorable one's gratified esteem when she discovered how expertly her wishes had been carried out, this person could not fail to notice that the Maiden Blank was also materially agitated when she distributed the contents of the dish before her.

"Will you, of your enlightened courtesy, accept, and overlook the deficiencies of, a portion of rabbit-pie, O high-souled Mr. Kong?" she inquired gracefully when this insignificant person was reached, and, concealing my many-hued emotion beneath an impassive face, I bowed agreeably as I replied, "To the beggar, black bread is a royal course."

"WHAT pie did you say, dear?" whispered another autumnal maiden, when all had partaken somewhat, and at her words a most consistently acute silence involved the table.

"I—I don't quite know," replied the one of the upper end, becoming excessively devoid of complexion; and restraining her voice she forthwith sent down an attending slave to inquire closely.

At this point a person of degraded ancestry endeavoured to remove the undoubted cloud of depression by feigning the nocturnal cry of the domestic cat; but in this he was not successful, and a maiden opposite, after fixedly regarding a bone on her plate, withdrew suddenly, embracing herself as she went. A moment later the slave returned, proclaiming aloud that the dish which had been prepared for the occasion had now been accidentally discovered by the round-bodied cook beneath the cushions of an arm-chair (a spot by no means satisfactory to this person's imagination had the opportunities at his disposal been more diffuse).

"What, then, is this of which we have freely partaken?" cried they around, and, in the really impressive silence which followed, an inopportune person discovered a small silver tablet among the fragments upon his plate, and, taking it up, read aloud the single word, "Influenza."

During the day, and even far into the uncounted gong-strokes of the time of darkness, this person had frequently remained in a fascinated contemplation of the moment when he should reveal himself and stand up to receive the benevolently-expressed congratulations of all who paid an agreed sum at fixed intervals, and, particularly, the dazzling though confessedly unsettling glance-thanks of the celestially-formed maiden who had explicitly stated that she was desirous of having a little dog. Now, however, when

13

this part of the enterprise ought to have taken place, I found myself unable to evade the conclusion that some important detail of the entire scheme had failed to agree harmoniously with the rest, and, had it been possible, I would have retired with unobtrusive tact and permitted another to wear my honourable acquirements. But, for some reason, as I looked around I perceived that every eye was fixed upon me with what at another time would have been a most engaging unanimity, and, although I bowed with undeterred profusion, and endeavoured to walk out behind an expression of all-comprehensive urbanity that had never hitherto failed me, a person of unsympathetic outline placed himself before the door, and two others, standing one on each side of me, gave me to understand that a recital of the full happening was required before I left the room.

It is hopeless to expect a display of refined intelligence at the hands of a people sunk in barbarism and unacquainted with the requirements of true dignity and the essentials of food preparation. On the manner of behaving of the male portion of those present this person has no inducement whatever to linger. Even the maiden for whom he had accomplished so much, after the nature of the misunderstanding had been made plain to her, uttered only a single word of approval, which, on subsequently consulting a book of interpretations, this person found to indicate: "A person of weak intellect; one without an adequate sense of the proportion and fitness of things; a buffoon; a jester; a compound of gooseberries scalded and crushed with cream"; but although each of these definitions may in a way be regarded as applicable, he is still unable to decide which was the precise one intended.

With salutations of filial regard, and in a spirit seven times refined by affliction and purified by vain regrets.

KONG HO. (Upon whose tablet posterity will perchance inscribe the titles, "Ill-destined but Misjudged.")

LETTER III

Concerning the virtuous amusements of both old and young.
The sit-round games. The masterpiece of the divine Li Tang,
and its reception by all, including that same Herbert.

VENERATED SIRE (whose breadth of mind is so well developed as
to take for granted boundless filial professions, which, indeed,
become vapid by a too frequent reiteration),—

Your amiable inquiry as to how the barbarians pass their time, when
not employed in affairs of commerce or in worshipping their
ancestors, has inspired me to examine the matter more fully. At the
same time your pleasantly-composed aphorism that the interior
nature of persons does not vary with the colour of their eyes, and
that if I searched I should find the old flying kites and the younger
kicking feather balls or working embroidery, according to their sex,
does not appear to be accurately sustained.

The lesser ones, it is true, engage in a variety of sumptuous
handicrafts, such as the scorching of wooden tablets with the
semblance of a pattern, and gouging others with sharpened
implements into a crude relief; depicting birds and flowers upon the
surface of plates, rending leather into shreds, and entwining beaten
iron, brass, and copper into a diversity of most ingenious
complications; but when I asked a maiden of affectionate and
domesticated appearance whether she had yet worked her age-
stricken father's coffin-cloth, she said that the subject was one upon
which she declined to jest, and rapidly involving herself in a profuse
display of emotion, she withdrew, leaving this one aghast.

To enable my mind to retranquillise, I approached a youth of
highly-gilded appearance, and, with many predictions of self-
inferiority, I suggested that we should engage in the stimulating
rivalry of feather ball. When he learned, however, that the diversion
consisted in propelling upwards a feather-trimmed chip by striking
it against the side of the foot, he candidly replied that he was afraid
he had grown out of shuttle-cock, but did not mind, if I was
vigorously inclined, "taking me on for a set of yang-pong."

15

Old men here, it is said, do not fly kites, and they affect to despise catching flies for amusement, although they frequently go fishing. Struck by this peculiarity, I put it in the form of an inquiry to one of venerable appearance, why, when at least five score flies were undeniably before his eyes, he preferred to recline for lengthy periods by the side of a stream endeavouring to snare creatures of whose existence he himself had never as yet received any adequate proof. Doubtless in my contemptible ignorance, however, I used some word inaccurately, for those who stood around suffered themselves to become amused, and the one in question replied with no pretence of amiable condescension that the jest had already been better expressed a hundred times, and that I would find the behind parts of a printed leaf called "Punch" in the bookcase. Not being desirous of carrying on a conversation of which I felt that I had misplaced the most highly rectified ingredient, I bowed repeatedly, and replied affably that wisdom ruled his left side and truth his right.

It was upon this same occasion that a young man of unprejudiced wide-mindedness, taking me aside, asserted that the matter had not been properly set forth when I was inquiring about kites. Both old and young men, he continued, frequently endeavoured to fly kites, even in the involved heart of the city. He had tried once or twice himself, but never with encouraging success, chiefly, he was told, because his paper was not good enough. Many people, he added, would not scruple to mislead me with evasive ambiguity on this one subject owing to an ill-balanced conception of what constituted true dignity, but he was unwilling that his countrymen should be thought by mine to be sunk into a deeper barbarism than actually existed.

His warning was not inopportune. Seated next to this person at a later period was a maiden from whose agreeably-poised lips had hitherto proceeded nothing but sincerity and fact. Watching her closely I asked her, as one who only had a languid interest either one way or the other, whether her revered father or her talented and richly-apparelled brothers ever spent their time flying kites about the city. In spite of a most efficient self-control her colour changed at my words, and her features trembled for a moment, but quickly reverting to herself she replied that she thought not; then—as though to subdue my suspicions more completely—that she was sure they did not, as the kites would certainly frighten the horses and the appointed watchmen of the street would not allow it. She confessed, however, with unassumed candour, that the immediate descendants of her sister were gracefully proficient in the art.

16

From this, great and enlightened one, you will readily perceive how misleading an impression might be carried away by a person scrupulously-intentioned but not continually looking both ways, when placed among a people endowed with the uneasy suspicion of the barbarian and struggling to assert a doubtful refinement. Apart from this, there has to be taken into consideration their involved process of reasoning, and the unexpectedly different standards which they apply to every subject.

At the house of the Maidens Blank, when the evening was not spent in listening to melodious voices and the harmony of stringed woods, it was usual to take part in sit-round games of various kinds. (And while it is on his brush this person would say with commendable pride that a well-trained musician among us can extort more sound from a hollow wooden pig, costing only a few cash, than the most skilful here ever attain on their largest instrument—a highly-lacquered coffin on legs, filled with bells and hidden springs, and frequently sold for a thousand taels.)

Upon a certain evening, at the conclusion of one sit-round game which involved abrupt music, a barrier of chairs, and the exhilarating possibility of being sat upon by the young and vivacious in their zeal, a person of the company turned suddenly to the one who is communicating with you and said enticingly, "Why did Birdcage Walk?"

Not judging from his expression that this was other than a polite inquiry on a matter which disturbed his repose, I was replying that the manifestation was undoubtedly the work of a vexatious demon which had taken up its abode in the article referred to, when another, by my side, cried aloud, "Because it envied Queen Anne's Gate"; and without a pause cast back the question, "Who carved The Poultry?"

In spite of the apparent simplicity of the demand it was received by all in an attitude of complicated doubt, and this person was considering whether he might not acquire distinction by replying that such an office fell by custom to the lot of the more austere Maiden Blank, when the very inadequate reply, "Mark Lane with St. Mary's Axe," was received with applause and some observations in a half-tone regarding the identity of the fowl.

By the laws of the sit-round games the one who had last spoken now proclaimed himself, demanding to know, "Why did Battersea Rise?" but the involvement was evidently superficial, for the maiden at whose memory this one's organs still vibrate ignobly at once replied, "Because it thought Clapham Common," in turn inquiring, "What made the Marble Arch?"

Although I would have willingly sacrificed to an indefinite extent to be furnished with the preconcerted watchword, so that I might have enlarged myself in the eyes of this consecrated being's unapproachable esteem, I had already decided that the competition was too intangible for one whose thoughts lay in well-defined parallel lines, and it fell to another to reply, "To hear Salisbury Court."

This, O my broad-minded ancestor of the first degree—an aimless challenge coupled with the name of one recognisable spot, replied to by the haphazard retort of another place, frequently in no way joined to it, was regarded as an exceptionally fascinating sit-round game by a company of elderly barbarians!

"What couldn't Walbrook?" it might be, and "Such Cheapside," would be deemed a praiseworthy solution. "When did King's Bench Walk?" would be asked, and to reply, "When Gray's Inn Road," covered the one with overpowering acclamation. "Bevis Marks only an Inner Circle at The Butts; why?" was a demand of such elaborate complexity that (although this person was lured out of his self-imposed restraint by the silence of all round, and submerging his intelligence to an acquired level, unobtrusively suggested, "Because Aylesbury ducks, perchance") it fell to the one propounding to announce, "Because St. John's Wood Shoot-up Hill."

Admittedly it is written, "When the shutter is fastened the girdle is loosened," but it is as truly said, "Not in the head, nor yet in the feet, but in the organs of digestion does wisdom reside," and even in jesting the middle course of neither an excessive pride nor an absolute weak-mindedness is to be observed. With what concrete pangs of acute mental distress would this person ever behold his immaculate progenitor taking part in a similar sit-round game with an assembly of worthy mandarins, the one asking questions of meaningless import, as "Why did they Hangkow?" and another replying in an equal strain of no consecutiveness, "In order to T'in Tung!"

At length a person who is spoken of as having formerly been the captain of a band of warriors turned to me with an unsuspected absence of ferocity and said, "Your countrymen are very proficient in the art of epigram, are they not, Mr. Kong? Will you not, in turn, therefore, favour us with an example?" Whereupon several maidens exclaimed with engaging high temper, "Oh yes; do ask us some funny Chinese riddles, Mr. Kong!"

"Assuredly there are among us many classical instances of the light sayings which require matching," I replied, gratified that I should have the opportunity of showing their superiority. "One, harmonious beyond the blend of challenge and retort, is as follows— 'The Phoenix embroidered upon the side of the shoe: When the shoe advances the Phoenix leaps forward.'"

"Oh!" cried several of the maidens, and from the nature of their glances it might reasonably be gathered that already they began to recognise the inferiority of their own sayings.

"Is that the question, or the answer, or both?" asked a youth of unfledged maturity, and to hide their conscious humiliation several persons allowed their faces to melt away.

"That which has been expressed," replied this person with an ungrudging toleration, "is the first or question portion of the contrast. The answer is that which will be supplied by your honourable condescension."

"But," interposed one of the maidens, "it isn't really a question, you know, Mr. Kong."

"In a way of regarding it, it may be said to be question, inasmuch as it requires an answer to establish the comparison. The most pleasing answer is that which shall be dissimilar in idea, and yet at the same time maintain the most perfect harmony of parallel thought," I replied. "Now permit your exceptional minds to wander in a forest of similitudes: 'The Phoenix embroidered upon the side of the shoe: When the shoe advances the Phoenix leaps forward.'"

"Oh, if that's all you want," said the one Herbert, who by an ill destiny chanced to be present, "'The red-hot poker held before the Cat's nose: When the poker advances the Cat leaps backwards.'"

"Oh, very good!" cried several of those around, "of course it naturally would. Is that right, Mr. Kong?"

"If the high-souled company is satisfied, then it must be, for there is no conclusive right or wrong—only an unending search for that which is most gem-set and resourceful," replied this person, with an

19

ever-deepening conviction of no enthusiasm towards the sit-round game. "But," he added, resolved to raise for a moment the canopy of a mind swan-like in its crystal many-sidedness, and then leave them to their own ineptitude, "for five centuries nothing has been judged equal to the solution offered by Li Tang. At the time he was presented with a three-sided banner of silk with the names of his eleven immediate ancestors embroidered upon it in seven colours, and his own name is still handed down in imperishable memory."

"Oh, do tell us what it was," cried many. "It must have been clever."

"'The Dragon painted upon the face of the fan: When the fan is shaken the Dragon flies upwards,'" replied this person.

It cannot be denied that this was received with an attitude of respectful melancholy strikingly complimentary to the wisdom of the gifted Li Tang. But whether it may be that the time was too short to assimilate the more subtle delicacies of the saying, or whether the barbarian mind is inherently devoid of true balance, this person was panged most internally to hear one say to another as he went out, "Do you know, I really think that Herbert's was much the better answer of the two—more realistic, and what you might expect at the pantomime." *

A like inability to grasp with a clear and uninvolved vision, permeates not only the triviality of a sit-round game but even the most important transactions of existence.

Shortly after his arrival in the Island, this person was initiated by the widely-esteemed Quang-Tsun into the private life of one whose occupation was that of a Law-giver, where he frequently drank tea on terms of mutual cordiality. Upon such an occasion he was one day present, conversing with the lesser ones of the household—the head thereof being absent, setting forth the Law in the Temple— when one of the maidens cried out with amiable vivacity, "Why, Mr. Kong, you say such consistently graceful things of the ladies you have met over here, that we shall expect you to take back an English wife with you. But perhaps you are already married in China?"

"The conclusion is undeviating in its accuracy," replied this person, unable to evade the allusion. "To Ning, Hia-Fa and T'ain Yen, as the matter stands."

"Ning Hia-Fa An T'ain Yen!" exclaimed the wife of the Law-giver pleasantly. "What an important name. Can you pardon our curiosity and tell us what she is like?"

"Ning, Hia-Fa AND T'ain Yen," repeated this person, not submitting to be deprived of the consequence of two wives without due protest. "Three names, three wives. Three very widely separated likes."

At this in no way boastfully uttered statement the agreeably outlined surface of the faces around variated suddenly, the effect being one which I have frequently observed in the midst of my politest expressions of felicity. For a moment, indeed, I could not disguise from myself that the one who had made the inquiry stretched forth her lotus-like hand towards the secret spring by which it is customary to summon the attending slaves from the underneath parts, but restraining herself with the manner of one who would desire to make less of a thing that it otherwise might seem, she turned to me again.

"How nice!" she murmured. "What a pity you did not bring them all with you, Mr. Kong. They would have been a great acquisition."

"Yet it must be well weighed," I replied, not to be out-complimented touching one another, "that here they would have met so many fine and superior gentlemen that they might have become dissatisfied with my less than average prepossessions."

"I wonder if they did not think of that in your case, and refuse to let you come," said one of the maidens.

"The various persons must not be regarded as being on their all fours," I replied, anxious that there should be no misunderstanding on this point. "They, of course, reside within one inner chamber, but there would be no duplicity in this one adding indefinitely to the number."

"Of course not; how silly of me!" exclaimed the maiden. "What splendid musical evenings you can have. But tell me, Mr. Kong (ought it not to be Messrs. Kong, mamma?), if a girl married you here would she be legally married to you in China?"

"Oh yes," replied this person positively.

"But could you not, by your own laws, have the marriage set aside whenever you wished?"

"Assuredly," I admitted. "It is so appointed."

21

"Then how could she be legally married?" she persisted, with really unbecoming suspicion.

"Legally married, legally unmarried," replied this person, quite distressed within himself at not being able to understand the difficulty besetting her. "All perfectly legal and honourably observed."

"I think, Gwendoline—" said the one of authority, and although the matter was no further expressed, by an instinct which he was powerless to avert, this person at once found himself rising with ceremonious partings.

Not desiring that the obstacle should remain so inadequately swept away, I have turned my presumptuous footsteps in the direction of the Law-giver's house on several later occasions, but each time the word of the slave guarding the door has been that they of the household, down even to those of the most insignificant degree of kinship, have withdrawn to a distant and secluded spot.

With renewed assurances that the enterprise is being gracefully conducted, however ill-digested and misleading these immature compositions may appear.

KONG HO.

22

LETTER IV

Concerning a desire to expatiate upon subjects of philosophical importance and its no accomplishment. Three examples of the mental concavity sunk into by these barbarians. An involved episode which had the outward appearance of being otherwise than what it was.

VENERATED SIRE (whose genial liberality on all necessary occasions is well remembered by this person in his sacrifices, with the titles "Benevolent" and "Open-sleeved"),—

I had it in my head at one time to tell you somewhat of the Classics most reverenced in this country, of the philosophical opinions which prevail, and to enlighten you generally upon certain other subjects of distinguished eminence. As the deities arranged, however, it chanced that upon my way to a reputable quarter of the city where the actuality of these matters can be learnt with the least evasion, my footsteps were drawn aside by an incident which now permeates my truth-laden brush to the exclusion of all else.

But in the first place, if it be permitted for a thoroughly untrustworthy son to take so presumptuous a liberty with an unvaryingly sagacious father, let this one entreat you to regard everything he writes in a very wide-headed spirit of looking at the matter from all round. My former letters will have readily convinced you that much that takes place here, even among those who can afford long finger-nails, would not be tolerated in Yuen-ping, and in order to avoid the suspicion that I am suffering from a serious injury to the head, or have become a prey to a conflicting demon, it will be necessary to continue an even more highly-sustained tolerant alertness. This person himself has frequently suffered the ill effects of rashly assuming that because he is conducting the adventure in a prepossessing spirit his efforts will be honourably received, as when he courteously inquired the ages of a company of maidens into whose presence he was led, and complimented the one whom he was desirous of especially gratifying by assuring her that she had every appearance of being at least twice the nine-and-twenty years to which she modestly laid claim.

23

Upon another occasion I entered a barber's stall, and finding it oppressively hot within, I commanded the attendant to carry a reclining stool into the street and there shave my lower limbs and anoint my head. As he hesitated to obey—doubtless on account of the trivial labour involved—I repeated my words in a tone of fuller authority, holding out the inducement of a just payment when he complied, and assuring him that he would certainly be dragged before the nearest mandarin and tortured if he held his joints stiffly. At this he evidently understood his danger, for obsequiously protesting that he was only a barber of very mean attainments, and that his deformed utensils were quite inadequate for the case, he very courteously directed me in inquire for a public chariot bound for a quarter called Colney Hatch (the place of commerce, it is reasonable to infer, of the higher class barbers), and, seating myself in it, instruct the attendant to put me down at the large gates, where they possessed every requisite appliance, and also would, if desirable, shave my head also. Here the incident assumes a more doubtful guise, for, notwithstanding the admitted politeness of the one who spoke, each of those to whom I subsequently addressed myself on the subject, presented to me a face quite devoid of encouragement. While none actually pointed out the vehicle I sought, many passed on in a state of inward contemplation without replying, and some—chiefly the attendants of other chariots of a similar kind—replied in what I deemed to be a spirit of elusive metaphor, as he who asserted that such a conveyance must be sought for at a point known intimately as the Aldgate Pump, whence it started daily at half-past the thirteenth gong-stroke; and another, who maintained that I had no prospect of reaching the desired spot until I secured the services of one of a class of female attendants who wear flowing blue robes in order to indicate that they are prepared to encounter and vanquish any emergency in life. To make no elaborate pretence in the matter this person may definitely admit that he never did reach the place in question, nor—in spite of a diligent search in which he has encountered much obloquy—has he yet found any barber sufficiently well equipped to undertake the detail.

Even more recently I suffered the unmerited rebuke of the superficial through performing an act of deferential politeness. Learning that the enlightened and magnanimous sovereign of this country was setting out on a journey I stationed myself in the forefront of those who stood before his palace, intending to watch such parts of the procession as might be fitly witnessed by one of my condition. When these had passed, and the chariot of the greatest approached, I respectfully turned my back to the road with a propitiatory gesture, as of one who did not deem himself worthy even to look upon a being of such majestic rank and acknowledged excellence. This delicate action, by some incredible process of mental obliquity, was held by those around to be a deliberate insult, if not even a preconcerted signal, of open treachery, and had not a heaven-sent breeze at that moment carried the hat of a very dignified bystander into the upper branches of an opportune tree, and successfully turned aside the attention of the assembly into a most immoderate exhibition of utter loss of gravity, I should undoubtedly have been publicly tortured, if not actually torn to pieces.

But the incident first alluded to was of an even more elaborately-contrived density than these, and some of the details are still unrolled before the keenest edge of this one's inner perception. Nevertheless, all is now set down in unbroken exactness for your impartial judgment.

At the time of this exploit I had only ventured out on a few occasions, and then, save those recorded, to no considerable extent; for it had already become obvious that the enterprises in which I persistently became involved never contributed to my material prosperity, and the disappointment of finding that even when I could remember nine words of a sentence in their language none of the barbarians could understand even so much as a tenth of my own, further cast down my enthusiasm.

On the day which has been the object of this person's narration from the first, he set out to become more fully instructed in the subjects already indicated, and proceeding in a direction of which he had no actual knowledge, he soon found himself in a populous and degraded quarter of the city. Presently, to his reasonable astonishment, he saw before him at a point where two ill-constructed thoroughfares met, a spacious and important building, many-storied in height, ornamented with a profusion of gold and crystal, marble and precious stones, and displaying from a tall pole the three-hued emblem of undeniable authority. A never-ending stream of people passed in and out by the numerous doors; the strains of expertly wielded instruments could be distinctly heard inside, and the warm odour of a most prepossessing spiced incense permeated the surroundings. "Assuredly," thought the person who is now recording the incident, "this is one of the Temples of barbarian worship"; and to set all further doubt at rest he saw in letters of gilt splendour a variety of praiseworthy and appropriate inscriptions, among which he read and understood, "Excellent," "Fine Old," "Well Matured," "Spirits only of the choicest quality within," together with many other invocations from which he could not wrest the hidden significance, as "Old Vatted," "Barclay's Entire," "An Ordinary at One," and the like.

By this time an impressive gathering had drawn around, and from its manner of behaving conveyed the suspicion that an entertainment or manifestation of some kind was confidently awaited. To disperse so outrageous a misconception this person was on the point of withdrawing himself when he chanced to see, over the principal door of the Temple, a solid gold figure of colossal magnitude, represented as crowned with leaves and tendrils, and holding in his outstretched hands a gigantic, and doubtless symbolic, bunch of grapes. "This," I said to myself, "is evidently the tutelary deity of the place, so displayed to receive the worship of the passer-by." With the discovery a thought of the most irreproachable benevolence possessed me. "Why should not this person," I reflected, "gain the unstinted approbation of those barbarians" (who by this time completely encircled me in) "by doing obeisance towards their deity, and by the same act delicately and inoffensively rebuke them for their own too-frequent intolerable attitude towards the susceptibilities of others? As an unprejudiced follower, in his own land, of the systems of Confucius, Lao-tse, and Buddha, this person already recognises the claims of seventeen thousand nine hundred and thirty-three deities of various grades, so that the addition of one more to that number can be a heresy of very trivial expiation." Inspired by these honourable sentiments, therefore, I at once prostrated myself on the ground, and, amid a silence of really illimitable expectation, I began to kow-tow repeatedly with ceremonious precision.

At this display of charitable broadmindedness an approving shout went up on all sides. Thus encouraged I proceeded to kow-tow with even more unceasing assiduousness, and presently words of definite encouragement mingled with the shout. "Do not flag in your amiable disinterestedness, Kong Ho," I whispered in my ear, "and out of your well-sustained endurance may perchance arise a cordial understanding, and ultimately a remunerative alliance between two distinguished nations." Filled with this patriotic hope I did not suffer my neck to stiffen, and doubtless I would have continued the undertaking as long as the sympathetic persons who hemmed me in signified their refined approval, when suddenly the cry was raised, "Look out, here comes the coppers!"

This, O my venerable-headed father, I at once guessed to be the announcement heralding the collecting-bowl which some over-zealous bystander was preparing to pass round on my behalf, doubtless under the impression—so obtuse in grasping the true relationship of events are many of the barbarians—that I was a wandering monk, displaying my reverence for the purpose of mendicancy. Not wishing to profit by this offensive misapprehension, I was preparing to rise, when a hand was unceremoniously laid upon my shoulder, and turning round I saw behind me one of the official watch—a class of men so powerful that at a gesture from their uplifted hands even the fiercest untamed horse will not infrequently stand upon its hind legs in mute submission.

"Early morning salutations," I said pleasantly, though somewhat involved in speech by my exertion (for these persons are ever to be treated with discriminating courtesy). "Prosperity to your house, O energetic street-watcher, and a thousand grandsons to worship their illustrious ancestor."

"Thanks," he replied concisely. "I'm a single man. As yet. Now then, will you make a way there? Can you stand?"

"Stand?" repeated this person, at once recognising one of the important words of inner meaning concerning which he had been initiated by the versatile Quang-Tsun. "Certainly this person will not hesitate to establish his footing if the exaction is thought to be desirable. Let us, therefore, bend our steps in the direction of a tea-house of unquestionable propriety."

"You've bent your steps into quite enough tea-houses, as you call them, for one day," replied the official with evasive meaning, at the same time assisting me to rise (for it need not be denied that the restrained position had made me for the moment incapable of a self-sustaining effort). "Look what you've done."

At the direction of his glance I cast my eyes along the street, east and west, and for the first time I became aware that what I had last seen as a reasonable gathering had now taken the proportions of an innumerable multitude which filled the entire space of the thoroughfare, while others covered the roofs above and protruded themselves from every available window. In our own land the

27

interspersal of umbrellas, musical instruments, and banners, with an occasional firework, would have given a greater animation to the scene; but with this exception I have never taken part in a more impressive and well-extended procession. Even while I looked, the helmets of other official watchers appeared in the distance, as immature junks upon the storm-tossed Whang-Hai, apparently striving fruitlessly to reach us.

As I was by no means sure what attitude was expected of me, I smiled with an all-embracing approval, and signified to the one at my side, by way of passing the time pleasurably together, that the likelihood of his nimble-witted friends reaching us with unruffled garments was remote in the extreme.

"Don't you let that worry you, Li Hung Chang," he said, in a tone that had the appearance of being outside itself around a deeper and more bitter significance; "if we get out again with any garments at all it won't be your fault. Why, you—well, YOU ought to have been put on the Black List long ago, by rights."

This, exalted one, although I have not yet been able to learn the exact dignity of it from any of the books of civil honours, is undoubtedly a mark of signal attainment, conferred upon the few for distinguishing themselves by some particular capacity; as our Double Dragon, for instance. Anxious to learn something of the privileges of the rank from one who evidently was not without influence in the bestowal, and not unwilling to show him that I was by no means of low-caste descent, I said to the official, "In his own country one of this person's ancestors wore the Decoration of the Yellow Scabbard, which entitled him to be carried in his chair up to the gate of the Forbidden Palace before descending to touch the ground. Is this Order of the Black List of a like purport?"

"You're right," he said, "it is. In this country it entitles you to be carried right inside the door at Bow Street without ever touching the ground. Look out! Now we shall not—"

At that moment what this person at first assumed to be a floral tribute, until he saw that not only the entire plant, but the earthenware jar also were attached, struck the official upon the helmet, whereupon, drawing a concealed club, he ceased speaking.

How the entertainment was conducted to such a development this person is totally inadequate to express; but in an incredibly short space of time the scene became one of most entrancing variety. From every visible point around the air became filled with commodities which—though doubtless without set intention—fittingly represented the arts, manufactures, and natural history of this resourceful country, all cast in prolific abundance at the feet of the official and myself, although the greater part inevitably struck our heads and bodies before reaching them. Beyond our immediate circle, as it may be expressed, the crowd never ceased to press forward with resistless activity, and among it could be seen occasionally the official watchmen advancing self-reliantly, though frequently without helmets, and, not less often, the helmets advancing without the official watchmen. To add to the acknowledged interest, every person present was proclaiming his views freely on a diversity of subjects, and above all could be heard the clear notes of the musical instruments by which the officials sought to encourage one another in their extremity, and to deaden the cries of those whom they outclubbed.

Despite this person's repeated protests that the distinction was too excessive, he was plucked from hand to hand irresistibly among those around, losing a portion of his ill-made attire at each step, so agreeably anxious were all to detain him. Just when the exploit seemed likely to have a disagreeable ending, however, he was thrust heavily against a door which yielded, and at once barring it behind him, he passed across the open space into which it led, along a passage between two walls, and thence through an involved labyrinth and beneath the waters of a canal into a wood of attractive seclusion. Here this person remained, spending the time in a profitable meditation, until the light withdrew and the great sky lantern had ascended. Then he cautiously crept forth, and after some further trivial episodes which chiefly concern the obstinate-headed slave guarding the outer door of a tea-house, an unintelligent maiden in the employment of one vending silk-embroidered raiment, the mercenary controller of a two-wheeled chariot and the sympathetic and opportune arrival of a person seated upon a funeral car, he succeeded in reaching the place of his abode.

With unalterable affection and a material request that an unstinted adequacy of new garments may be sent by a sure and speedy hand.

KONG HO.

*Concerning the neglect of ancestors and its discreditable
consequences. Two who state the matter definitely.
Concerning the otherside way of looking at things and the
self-contradictory bearing of the maiden Florence.*

VENERATED SIRE,—A discovery of overwhelming malignity
oppresses me. In spite of much baffling ambiguity and the frequent
evasion of conscious guilt, there can be no longer any reasonable
doubt that these barbarians DO NOT WORSHIP THEIR
ANCESTORS!

Hitherto the matter had rested in my mind as an uneasy breath of
suspicion, agitated from time to time by countless indications that
such a possibility might, indeed, exist in a condensed form, but too
inauspiciously profane to be contemplated in the altogether. Thus,
when in the company of the young this person has walked about the
streets of the city, he may at length have said, "Truly, out of your
amiable condescension, you have shown me a variety of entrancing
scenes. Let us now in turn visit the tombs of your ancestors, to the
end that I may transmit fitting gifts to their spirits and discharge a
few propitious fireworks as a greeting." Yet in no case has this well-
intentioned offer been agilely received, one asserting that he did not
know the resting-place of the tombs in question, a second that he
had no ancestors, a third that Kensal Green was not an entrancing
spot for a wet afternoon, a fourth that he would see them removed
to a greater distance first, another that he drew the line at
mafficking in a cemetery, and the like. These things, it may occur to
your omniscience, might in themselves have been conclusive, yet
the next reference to the matter would perhaps be tending to a more
alluring hope.

"To-morrow," a person has remarked in the hearing of this one, "I
go to the Stratford which is upon the Avon, and without a pause I
shall prostrate myself intellectually before the immortal
Shakespeare's tomb and worship his unequalled memory."

"The intention is benevolently conceived," I remarked. "Yet has he no descendants, this same Shakespeare, that the conciliation of his spirit must be left to chance?"

When he assured me that this calamity had come about, I would have added a richly-gilded brick from my store for transmission also, in the hope that the neglected and capricious shadow would grant me an immunity from its resentful attention, but the one in question raised a barrier of dissent. If I wished to adorn a tomb, he added (evading the deeper significance of the act), there was that of Goldsmith within its Temple, upon which many impressionable maidens from across the Bitter Waters of the West make it a custom to deposit chaplets of verses, in the hope of seeing the offering chronicled in the papers; and in the Open Space called Trafalgar there were the images of a great captain who led many junks to victory and the Emperor of a former dynasty, where doubtless the matter could be arranged; but the surrounding had by this time become too involved, and this person had no alternative but to smile symmetrically and reply that his words were indeed opals falling from a topaz basin.

Later in the day, being desirous of becoming instructed more definitely, I addressed myself to a venerable person who makes clean the passage of the way at a point not far distant.

"If you have no sons to extend your industrious line," I said, when he had revealed this fact to me, "why do you not adopt one to that end?"

With narrow-minded covetousness, he replied that nowadays he had enough to do to keep himself, and that it would be more reasonable to get some one to adopt HIM.

"But," I exclaimed, ignoring this ill-timed levity, "who, when you have Passed Beyond, will worship you and transmit to your spirit the necessities of life?"

"Governor," he replied, using the term of familiar dignity, "I've made shift without being worshipped for five and sixty years, and it worries me a sight more to know who will transmit to my body the necessities of life until I HAVE Passed Beyond."

"The final consequences of your self-opinionated carelessness," this person continued, "will be that your neglected and unprovided shadow, finding itself no longer acceptable to the society of the better class demons, will wander forth, and allying itself in despair

31

to the companionship of a band of outcasts like itself, will be driven to dwell in unclean habitations and to subsist on the uncertain bounty of the charitable."

"Very likely," replied the irredeemable person before me. "I can't help its troubles. I have to do all that myself as it is."

Doubtless this fanaticism contains the secret of the ease with which these barbarians have possessed themselves of the greater part of the earth, and have even planted their assertive emblems on one or two spots in our own Flowery Kingdom. What, O my esteemed parent, what can a brave but devout and demon-fearing nation do when opposed to a people who are quite prepared to die without first leaving an adequate posterity to tend their shrines and offer incense? Assuredly, as a neighbouring philosopher once had occasion to remark, using for his purpose a metaphor so technically-involved that I must leave the interpretation until we meet, "It may be war, but it isn't cricket."

The inevitable outcome, naturally, is that the Island must be the wandering-place of myriads of spirits possessing no recognised standing, and driven by want—having none to transmit them offerings—to the most degraded subterfuges. It is freely admitted that there is scarcely an ancient building not the abode of one or more of these abandoned demons, doubtless well-disposed in the first instance, and capable of becoming really beneficent Forces until they were driven to despair by obstinate neglect. A society of very honourable persons (to which this one has unobtrusively contributed a gift), exists for the purpose of searching out the most distressing and meritorious cases among them, and removing them, where possible, to a more congenial spot. The remarkable fact, to this person's mind, is, that with the air and every available space around absolutely packed with demons (as certainly must be the prevailing state of things), the manifestations of their malignity and vice are, if anything, rather less evident here than in our own favoured country, where we do all in our power to satisfy their wants.

That same evening I found myself seated next to a maiden of prepossessing vivacity, who was spoken of as being one of a kindred but not identical race. Filled with the incredible profanity of those around, and hoping to find among a nation so alluringly high-spirited a more congenial elevation of mind, I at length turned to her and said, "Do not regard the question as one of unworthy curiosity, for this person's inside is white and funereal with his fears; but do you, of your allied race, worship your ancestors?"

The maiden spent a moment in conscientious thought. "No, Mr. Kong," she replied, with a most commendable sigh of unfeigned regret, "I can't say that we do. I guess it's because we're too new. Mine, now, only go back two generations, and they were mostly in lard. If they were old and baronial it might be different, but I can't imagine myself worshipping an ancestor in lard." (This doubtless refers to some barbaric method of embalming.)

"And your wide and enlightened countrymen?" I asked, unable to restrain a passion of pure-bred despair. "Do they also so regard the obligation?"

"I am afraid so," replied the maiden, with an honourable indication towards my emotion. "But of course when a girl marries into the European aristocracy, she and all her folk worship her husband's ancestors, until every one about is fairly dizzy with the subject."

It is largely owing to the graceful and virtuous conversation of these lesser ones that this person's knowledge of the exact position which the ceremonial etiquette of the country demands on various occasions is becoming so proficiently enlarged. It is true that they of my own sex do not hesitate to inquire with penetrating assiduousness into certain of the manners and customs of our land, but these for the most part do not lead to a conversation in any way profitable to my discreeter understanding. Those of the inner chamber, on the other hand, while not scrupling to question me on the details of dress, the braiding and gumming of the hair, the style and variety of the stalls of merchants, the wearing of jade, gold, and crystal ornaments and flowers about the head, smoking, and other matters affecting our lesser ones, very magnanimously lead my contemplation back to a more custom-established topic if by any hap in my ambitious ignorance I outstep it.

In such a manner it chanced on a former occasion that I sat side by side with a certain maiden awaiting the return of others who had withdrawn for a period. The season was that of white rains, and the fire being lavishly extended about the grate we had harmoniously arranged ourselves before it, while this person, at the repeated and explicit encouragement of the maiden, spoke openly of such details of the inner chamber as he has already indicated.

"Is it true, Mr. Ho" (thus the maiden, being unacquainted with the actual facts, consistently addressed me), "that ladies' feet are relentlessly compressed until they finally assume the proportions and appearance of two bulbs?" and as she spoke she absent-mindedly regarded her own slippers, which were out-thrust somewhat to receive the action of the fire.

"It is a matter which cannot reasonably be denied," I replied; "and it is doubtless owing to this effect that they are designated 'Golden Lilies.' Yet when this observance has been slowly and painfully accomplished, the extremities in question are not less small but infinitely less graceful than the select and naturally-formed pair which this person sees before him." And at the ingeniously-devised compliment (which, not to become large-headed in self-imagination, it must be admitted was revealed to me as available for practically all occasions by the really invaluable Quang-Tsun), I bowed unremittingly.

"O, Mr. Ho!" exclaimed the maiden, and paused abruptly at the sound of her words, as though they were inept.

"In many other ways a comparison equally irreproachable to the exalted being at my side might be sought out," I continued, suddenly forming the ill-destined judgment that I was no less competent than the more experienced Quang-Tsun to contrive delicate offerings of speech. "Their hair is rope like in its lack of spontaneous curve, their eyes as deficient in lustre as a half-shuttered window; their hands are exceedingly inferior in colour, and both on the left side, as it may be expressed; their legs—" but at this point the maiden drew herself so hastily into herself that I had no alternative but to conclude that unless I reverted in some way the enterprise was in peril of being inharmoniously conducted.

"Mr. Ho," said the maiden, after contemplating her inward thoughts for a moment, "you are a foreigner, and you cannot be expected to know by instinct what may and what may not be openly expressed in this country. Therefore, although the obligation is not alluring, I think it kinder to tell you that the matters which formed the subject of your last words are never to be referred to."

At this rebuke I again bowed persistently, for it did not appear reasonable to me that I could in any other way declare myself without violating the imposed command.

"Not only are they never openly referred to," continued the maiden, who in spite of the declared no allurement of the subject did not

34

seem disposed to abandon it at once, "but among the most select they are, by unspoken agreement, regarded as 'having no actual existence,' as you yourself would say."

"Yet," protested this person, somewhat puzzled, "to one who has witnessed the highly-achieved attitudes of those within your Halls of Harmony, and in an unyielding search for knowledge has addressed himself even to the advertisement pages of the ladies' papers—"

The maiden waved her hand magnanimously. "In your land, as you have told me, there are many things, not really existing, which for politeness you assume to be. In a like but converse manner this is to be so regarded."

I thanked her voluminously. "The etiquette of this country is as involved as the spoken tongue," I said, "for both are composed chiefly of exceptions to a given rule. It was formerly impressed upon this person, as a guiding principle, that that which is unseen is not to be discussed; yet it is not held in disrepute to allude to so intimate and secluded an organ as the heart, for no further removed than yesterday he heard the deservedly popular sea-lieutenant in the act of declaring to you, upon his knees, that you were utterly devoid of such a possession."

At this inoffensively-conveyed suggestion, the fire opposite had all the appearance of suddenly reflecting itself into the maiden's face with a most engaging concentration, while at the same time she stamped her foot in ill-concealed rage.

"You've been listening at the door!" she cried impetuously, "and I shall never forgive you."

"To no extent," I declared hastily (for although I had indeed been listening at the door, it appeared, after the weight which she set upon the incident, more honourable that I should deny it in order to conciliate her mind). "It so chanced that for the moment this person had forgotten whether the handle he was grasping was of the push-out or turn-in variety, and in the involvement a few words of no particular or enduring significance settled lightly upon his perception.

"In that case," she replied in high-souled liberality, while her eyes scintillated towards me with a really all-overpowering radiance, "I will forgive you."

35

"We have an old but very appropriate saying, 'To every man the voice of one maiden carries further than the rolling of thunder,'" I remarked in a significantly restrained tone; for, although conscious that the circumstance was becoming more menace-laden than I had any previous intention, I found myself to be incapable of extrication. "Florence—"

"Oh," she exclaimed quickly, raising her polished hand with an undeniable gesture of reproof, "you must not call me by my christian name, Mr. Ho."

"Yet," replied this person, with a confessedly stubborn inelegance, "you call me by the name of Ho."

Her eyes became ox-like in an utter absence of almond outline. "Yes," she said gazing, "but that—that is not your christian name, is it?"

"In a position of speaking—this one being as a matter of fact a discreditable follower of the sublime Confucius—it may be so regarded," I answered, "inasmuch as it is the milk-name of childhood."

"But you always put it last," she urged.

"Assuredly," I replied. "Being irrevocably born with the family name of Kong, it is thought more reasonable that that should stand first. After that, others are attached as the various contingencies demand it, as Ho upon participating in the month-age feast, the book-name of Tsin at a later period, Paik upon taking a degree, and so forth."

"I am very sorry, Mr. Kong," said the maiden, adding, with what at the time certainly struck this person as shallow-witted prejudice. "Of course it is really quite your own fault for being so tospy-turvily arranged in every way. But, to return to the subject, why should not one speak of one's heart?"

"Because," replied this person, colouring deeply, and scarcely able to control his unbearable offence that so irreproachably-moulded a creature should openly refer to the detail, "because it is a gross and unrefined particular, much more internal and much less pleasantly-outlined than those extremities whose spoken equivalent shall henceforth be an abandoned word from my lips."

"But, in any case, it is not the actual organ that one infers,"

36

protested the maiden. "As the seat of the affections, passions, virtues, and will, it is the conventional emblem of every thought and emotion."

"By no means," I cried, forgetting in the face of so heterodox an assertion that it would be well to walk warily at every point. "That is the stomach."

"Ah!" exclaimed the maiden, burying her face in a gracefully-perfumed remnant of lace, to so overwhelming a degree that for the moment I feared she might become involved in the dizzy falling. "Never, by any mischance, use that word again the society of the presentable, Mr. Kong."

"The ceremonial usage of my own land of the Heavenly Dynasty is proverbially elaborate," I said, with a gesture of self-abasement, "but in comparison with yours it may be regarded as an undeviating walk when opposed to a stately and many-figured dance. Among the company of the really excessively select (in which must ever be included the one whom I am now addressing), it becomes difficult for an outcast of my illimitable obtuseness to move to one side or the other without putting his foot into that."

"Oh no," exclaimed the maiden, in fragrant encouragement, "I think you are getting on very nicely, Mr. Kong, and one does not look for absolute conformance from a foreigner—especially one who is so extremely foreign. If I can help you with anything—of course I could not even speak as I have done to an ordinary stranger, but with one of a distant race it seems different—if I can tell you anything that will save you—"

"You are all-exalted," I replied, with seemly humility, "and virtue and wisdom press out your temples on either side. Certainly, since I have learned that the heart is so poetically regarded, I have been assailed by a fear lest other organs which I have hitherto despised might be used in a similar way. Now, as regards liver—"

"It is only used with bacon," replied the maiden, rising abruptly.

"Kidneys?" suggested this person diffidently, really anxious to detain her footsteps, although from her expression it did not rest assured that the incident was taking an actually auspicious movement.

"I don't think you need speak of those except at breakfast," she said;

"but I hear the others returning, and I must really go to dress for dinner."

Among the barbarians many keep books wherein to inscribe their deep and beautiful thoughts. This person had therefore provided himself with one also, and, drawing it forth, he now added to a page of many other interesting compositions: "Maidens of immaculate refinement do not hesitate to admit before a person of a different sex that they are on the point of changing their robes. The liver is in some intricate way an emblem representing bacon, or together with it the two stand for a widely differing analogy. Among those of the highest exclusiveness kidneys are never alluded to after the tenth gong-stroke of the morning."

With a sincerely ingrained trust that the scenes of dignity, opulence, and wisdom, set forth in these superficial letters, are not unsettling your intellect and causing you to yearn for a fuller existence.

KONG HO.

LETTER VI

Concerning this person's well-sustained efforts to discover further demons. The behaviour of those invoked on two occasions.

VENERATED SIRE,—In an early letter I made some reference to a variety of demon invoked by certain of the barbarians. As this matter aroused your congenial interest, I have since privately bent my mind incessantly to the discovery of others; but this has been by no means easy, for, touching the more intimate details of the subject, the barbarians frequently maintain a narrow-minded suspicion. Many whom I have approached feign to become amused or have evaded a deliberate answer under the subterfuge of a jest; yet, whenever I would have lurked by night in their temples or among the enclosed spaces of their tombs to learn more, at a given signal one in authority has approached me with anxiety and mistrust engraved upon his features, and, disregarding my unassuming protest that I would remain alone in a contemplative reverie, has signified that so devout an exercise is contrary to their written law.

On one occasion only did this person seem to hold himself poised on the very edge of a fuller enlightenment. This was when, in the venerable company of several benevolent persons, he was being taken from place to place to see the more important buildings, and to observe the societies of artificers labouring at their crafts. The greater part of the day had already been spent in visiting temples, open spaces reserved to children and those whose speech, appearance, and general manner of behaving make it desirable that they should be set apart from the contact of the impressionable, halls containing relics and emblems of the past, places of no particular size or attraction but described as being of unparalleled historic interest, and the stalls of the more reputable venders of merchandise.

Doubtless, with observing so many details of a conflicting nature, this person's discriminating faculties had become obscured, but

39

towards evening he certainly understood that we sought the company of an assembly of those who had been selected from all the Empire to pronounce definitely upon matters of supreme import. The building before which our chariot stopped had every appearance of being worthy of so exceptional a gathering, and with a most affluent joy that I should at last be able to glean a decisive pronouncement, I evaded those who had accompanied me, and, mingling self-reliantly with the throng inside, I quickly surrounded myself with many of the wisest-looking, and begged that they would open their heads freely and express their innermost opinions upon the subject of demons of all kinds.

Although I had admittedly hoped that these persons would not conceal themselves behind the wings of epigram or intangible prevarication, I was far from being prepared for the candour with which they greeted me, and although by long usage I am reasonably unconcerned at the proximity of any of our own recognised genii, it is not to be denied that my organs of ferocity grew small and unstable at the revelations.

From their words it appeared that the spot on which we stood had long been the recognised centre and meeting-place for every class of abandoned and objectionable spirit of the universe. Not only this, but several of the persons who had gathered around were confidently pointed out as the earthly embodiment of various diabolical Forces, while others cheerfully admitted that they themselves were the shadows of certain illustrious ones who had long Passed Above, and all united in declaring that those who moved among them wearing the distinction of a dark blue uniform were Evil Beings of a most ghoulish and repulsive type. Indeed, as I looked more closely, I could see that not only those pointed out, but all standing around, had expressions immeasurably more in keeping with a band of outcast spirits than suggestive of an assembly representing wisdom and dignified ease. At that moment, however, a most inelegant movement was caused by one suddenly declaring that he had recognised this one who is inscribing his experiences to be the apparition of a certain great reformer who during the period of his ordinary existence had received the name of Guy Fawkes, and amid a tumult of overwhelming acclamation a proposal was raised that I should be carried around in triumph and afterwards initiated into the observance of a time-honoured custom. Although it had now become doubtful to what end the adventure was really tending, this person would have submitted himself agreeably to the participation had not the blue-apparelled band cleft their way into the throng just as I was about to be borne off in triumph, and forming themselves into a ringed barrier around me they presently succeeded in rearranging the contending elements and in restoring me to the society of my friends. To these persons they complained with somewhat unreasoning acrimony that I had been exciting the inmates into a state of rebellion with wild imaginings, and for the first time I then began to understand that an important error had been perpetrated by some one, and that instead of being a meeting-place for those upholding the wisdom and authority of the country, the building was in reality an establishment for the mentally defective and those of treacherous instincts.

For some time after this occurrence I failed to regard the subject of demons and allied Forces in any but a spirit of complete no enthusiasm, but more recently my interest and research have been enlarged by the zeal and supernatural conversation of a liberal-minded person who sought my prosaic society with indefatigable persistence. When we had progressed to such a length that the one might speak of affairs without the other at once interposing that he himself had also unfortunately come out quite destitute of money, this stranger, who revealed to me that his name was Glidder, but that in the company of a certain chosen few he was known intimately as the Keeper of the Salograma, approached me confidentially, and inquired whether we of our Central Kingdom were in the habit of receiving manifestations from the spirits of those who had Passed Beyond.

At the unassumed ingenuousness of this remark I suffered my impassiveness to relax, as I replied with well-established pride that although a country which neglected its ancestors might doubtless be able to produce more of the ordinary or graveyard spectres, we were unapproachable for the diverse forms and malignant enmity of our apparitions. Of invisible beings alone, I continued tolerantly, we had the distinction of being harassed by upwards of seven hundred clearly-defined varieties, while the commoner inflictions of demons, shades, visions, warlocks, phantoms, sprites, imps, phenomena, ghosts, and reflections passed almost without comment; and touching our admitted national speciality of dragons, the honour of supremacy had never been questioned.

At this, the agreeable person said that the pleasure he derived from meeting me was all-excelling, and that I must certainly accompany

41

him to a meeting-place of this same chosen few the following evening, when, by the means of sacred expedients, they hoped to invoke the presence of some departed spirits, and perchance successfully raise a tangible vision or two. To so fair-minded a proposal I held myself acquiescently, and then inquired where the meeting-place in question was destined to be—whether in a ruined and abandoned sanctuary, or upon some precipitous spot of desolation.

The inquiry was gracefully intended, but a passing cloud of unworthy annoyance revealed itself upon the upper part of the other's expression as he replied, "We, the true seekers, despise theatrical accessories, and, as a matter of act, I couldn't well get away from the office in time to go anywhere far. To-morrow we meet at my place in the Camden Road. It's only a three-half-penny tram stage from the Euston and Tottenham Court corner, so it couldn't be much more convenient for you." He thereupon gave me an inscribed fragment of paper and mentioned the appointed hour.

"I'll tell you why I am particularly anxious for you to come to-morrow," he said as we were each departing from one another. "Pash—he's the Reader of the Veda among us—and his people have got hold of a Greek woman (they SAY she is a princess, of course), who can do a lot of things with flowers and plate glass. They are bringing her for the first time to-morrow, and it struck me that if I have YOU there already when they arrive—you'll come in your national costume by the way?—it will be a considerable set-off. Since his daughter was presented to the duchess at the opening of a bazaar, there has been no holding Pash; why he was ever elected Reader of the Books, I don't know. Er—we have had scoffers sometimes, but I trust I may rely upon you not to laugh at anything you may not happen to agree with?"

With conscientious dignity I replied that I had only really laughed seven times in my life, and therefore the entertainment was one which I was not likely to embark upon hastily or with inadequate cause. He immediately expressed a seemly regret that the detail had been spoken, and again assuring him that at the stated hour I would present myself at the house bearing the symbol engraved upon the card, we definitely parted.

That, as a matter of fact, I did not so present myself at the exact hour, chiefly concerns the uncouth and arbitrary-minded charioteer

42

who controlled the movements of the vehicle to which the one whom I was seeking had explicitly referred; for at an angle in the road he suffered the horses to draw us aside into a path which did not correspond to the engraved signs upon the card, nor by any word of persuasion could he be prevailed upon to return.

Thus, without any possible reproach upon the manner in which I was conducting the enterprise, it came about that by the time I reached the spot indicated, all those persons who had been spoken of as constituting a chosen band were assembled, and with them the barbarian princess. Nevertheless, this person was irreproachably greeted, and the maiden indicated even spoke a few words to him in an outside tongue. Being necessarily unacquainted with the import of the remark I spread out my hands with a sign of harmonious sympathy and smiled agreeably, whereat she appeared to receive an added esteem from the faces of those around (excluding those directly of the House of Glidder), and was thereby encouraged to speak similarly at intervals, this person each time replying in a like fashion.

"Is he then a Guide of the Way, also, princess?" said the one Pash, who had noted the occurrence; to which the maiden replied, "To a degree, yet lacking the Innermost Mysteries."

Presently it was announced that all things were fittingly prepared in another chamber. Here, upon a table of polished wood, stood on the one side a round stone with certain markings, a group of inscribed books, and various other emblems; and on the other side a bowl of water, a sphere of crystal, pieces of unwritten parchment, and behind all, and at a distance away, a sheet of transparent glass, greater in height than an ordinary person and as wide. When all were seated—the one who had enticed me among them placing himself before the stone, the person Pash guarding the books, the barbarian princess being surrounded by her symbols and alone in a self-imposed solitude, and the others at various points—the lights were subdued and the appearances awaited.

It would scarcely be respectful, O my enlightened father, to take up your well-spent leisure by a too prolific account of the matters which followed, they being in no way dissimilar from the manifestations by which the uninitiated little ones of Yuen-ping are wont to amuse themselves and pass the winter evenings. From time to time harmonious sounds could be plainly detected, flowers and branches of wood were scattered sparsely here and there, persons claimed that passing objects had touched their faces, and misshapen forms of smoke-like density (which some confidently recognised as the outlines of departed ones whom they had known), revealed themselves against the glass. When this had been accomplished, the lights were recalled, and the barbarian maiden, sinking into a condition of languor, announced and foretold events and happenings upon which she was consulted, sometimes replying by spoken words, at others suffering her hand to trace them lightly upon the parchment sheets. Thus, to an inquirer it was announced that one, Aunt Mary, in the Upper Air, was well and happy, though undeniably pained at the action of Cousin William in the matter of the freehold houses, and more than sceptical how his marriage would turn out. Another was advised that although the interest on Consols was admittedly lower than that anticipated by those controlling the destines of a new venture entitled, The Great Rosy Dawn Gold Mine Development Syndicate, and the name certainly less poetically inspiring, the advising spirits were of the opinion that the former enterprise would prove the more stable of the two, and, in any case, they recommended the person in question to begin by placing not more than half of her life's savings into the mine. The family of the House of Pash was assured that beneficent spirits surrounded them at every turn, and that their good deeds were not suffered to fall unfruitfully to the ground; while many bearing the name of Glidder, on the other hand, were reproved by one who had known them in infancy for the offences of jealousy, ostentation, vain thoughts, shallowness of character, and the like.

At length, revered, as there seemed to be no reasonable indication of any barbarian phantom of weight or authority appearing— nothing, indeed, beyond what a person in our country, of no admitted skill, would accomplish in the penetrating light of day with two others holding his hands, and a third reposing upon his head, I formed the perhaps immature judgment that the one to whom I was indebted for the entertainment would be suffering a grievous frustration of his hopes and a diminution of his outward authority. Therefore, without sufficient consideration of the restricted surroundings, as it afterwards appeared, I threw myself into a retrospective vision, and floating unencumbered through space, I sought for Kwan Kiang-ti, the Demon of the Waters, upon whom I might fittingly call, as I was given into his keeping by the ceremony of spirit-adoption at an early age. Meeting an influence which I recognised to be an indication of his presence, in the vicinity of the Eighth Region, I obsequiously entreated that he would reveal himself without delay, and then, convinced of his sympathetic intervention, I suffered my spirit to recall itself, and revived into the condition of an ordinary existence.

"We have among us this evening, my friends," the one Pash was saying, "a very remarkable lady—if I may use so democratic a term in the connection—to whom the limits of Time and Space are empty words, and before whose supreme Will the most portentous Forces of Occult Nature mutely confess themselves her attending slaves—" But at that moment the rolling drums of Kiang-ti's thunder drowned his words, although he subsequently raised his voice above it to entreat that any knives or other articles of a bright and attractive kind should at once be removed to a place of safety.

Heralded by these continuous sounds, and accompanied by innumerable flashes of lightning, the genius presently manifested himself, leisurely developing out of the air around. He appeared in his favourite guise of an upright dragon, his scales being arranged in rows of nine each way, a pearl showing within his throat, and upon his head the wooden bar. The lights were extinguished incapably by the rain which fell continually in his presence, but from his body there proceeded a luminous breath which sufficiently revealed the various incidents.

"Kong Ho," said this opportune vision, speaking with a voice like the beating of a brass gong, "the course you have adopted is an unusual one, but the weight and regularity of your offerings have merit in my eyes. Nevertheless, if your invocation is only the outcome of a shallow vanity or a profane love of display, nothing can save you from a painful death. Speak now, fully and without evasion, and fear nothing."

"Amiable Being," said this person, kow-towing profoundly, "the matter was designed to the end only that your incomparable versatility might be fittingly displayed. These barbarians sought vainly to raise phantoms capable of any useful purpose, whereupon I, jealous of your superior omnipotence, judged it would be an unseemly neglect not to inform you of the opportunity."

"It is well," said the demon affably. "All doubt in the matter shall now be set at rest. Could any more convincing act be found than that I should breath upon these barbarians and reduce them instantly to a scattering of thin white ashes?"

"Assuredly it would be a conclusive testimony," I replied; "yet in that case consider how inadequate a witness could be borne to your enlightened condescension, when none would be left but one to whom the spoken language of this Island is more in the nature of a trap than a comfortable vehicle."

"Your reasoning is profound, Kong Ho," he replied, "yet abundant proof shall not be wanting." With these words he raised his hand, and immediately the air became filled with an overwhelming shower of those productions with which Kwan Kiang-ti's name is chiefly associated—shells and pebbles of all kinds, lotus and other roots from the river banks, weeds from seas of greater depths, fish of interminable variety from both fresh and bitter waters, all falling in really embarrassing abundance, and mingled with an incessant rain of sand and water. In the midst of this the demon suddenly passed away, striking the table as he went, so that it was scarred with the brand of a five-clawed hand, shattering all the objects upon it (excepting the stone and the books, which he doubtless regarded as sacred to some extent), and leaving the room involved in a profound darkness.

"For the love av the saints—for the love av the saints, save us from the yellow devils!" exclaimed a voice from the spot where last the barbarian princess had reclined, and upon this person going to her assistance with lights it was presently revealed that she alone had remained seated, the others having all assembled themselves beneath the table in spite of the incapability of the space at their disposal. Most of the weightier evidences of Kwan Kiang-ti's majestic presence had faded away, though the table retained the print of his impressive hand, many objects remained irretrievably torn apart, and in a distant corner of the room an insignificant heap of shells and seaweed still lingered. From the floor covering a sprinkling of the purest Fuh-chow sand rose at every step, the salt dew of the Tung-Hai still dropped from the surroundings, and, at a later period, a shore crab was found endeavouring to make its escape undetected.

Convinced that the success of the manifestation would have enlarged the one Glidder's esteem towards me to an inexpressible degree, I now approached him with words of self-deprecation ready

46

on my tongue, but before he spoke I became aware, from the nature of his glance, that the provision had been unnecessary, for already his face had begun to assume, to a most distended amount, the expression which I had long recognised as a synonym that some detail had been regarded at a different angle from that anticipated.

"May I ask," he began in a somewhat heavily-laden voice, after he had assured himself that the person who was speaking was himself, and his external attributes unchanged, "May I ask, sir" (and at this title, which is untranslatable in its many-sided significance when technically employed, I recognised that all complimentary intercourse might be regarded as having closed), "whether you accept the responsibility of these proceedings?"

"Touching the appearance which has so essentially contributed to the success of the occasion, it is undeniably due to this one's foresight," I replied modestly.

"Then let me tell you, sir, that I consider it an outrage—a dastardly outrage."

"Yet," protested this person with retiring assertiveness, "the expressed object of the ceremony, as it stood before my intelligence, was for the set purpose of invoking spirits and raising certain visions."

"Spirits!" exclaimed the one before me with an accent of concentrated aversion; "yes, spirits; impalpable, civilised, genuine spirits, who manifest themselves through recognised media, and are conformable to the usages of the best drawing-room society—yes. But not demons, sir; not Chinese devils in the Camden Road—no. Truth and Light at any cost, not paganism. It's perfectly scandalous. Look at the mahogany table—ruined; look at the wall-paper—conventional mackerels with a fishing-net background, new this spring—soused; look at the Brussels carpet, seventeen six by twenty-five—saturated!"

"I quite agree with you, Mr. Glidder," here interposed the individual Pash. "I was watching you, sir, closely the whole time, and I have my suspicions about how it was done. I don't know whether Mr. Glidder has any legal redress, but I should certainly advise him to see his solicitors to-morrow, and in the meantime—"

"He is my guest," exclaimed the one whose hospitality I was enjoying, "and while he is beneath my roof he is sacred."

"But I do not think that it would be kind to detain him any longer in his wet things," said another of the household, with pointed malignity, and accepting this as an omen of departure, I withdrew myself, bowing repeatedly, but offering no closer cordiality.

"Through a torn sleeve one drops a purse of gold," it is well said; and as if to prove to a deeper end that misfortune is ever double-handed, this incapable being, involved in thoughts of funereal density, bent his footsteps to an inaccurate turning, and after much wandering was compelled to pass the night upon a desolate heath—but that would be the matter of another narrative.

With an insidious doubt whether, after all, the far-seeing Kwan Kiang-ti's first impulse would not have been the most satisfactory conclusion to the enterprise.

KONG HO.

LETTER VII

Concerning warfare, both as waged by ourselves and by a nation devoid of true civilisation. The aged man and the meeting and the parting of our ways. The instance of the one who expressed emotion by leaping.

VENERATED SIRE,—You are omniscient, but I cannot regard the fear which you express in your beautifully-written letter, bearing the sign of the eleventh day of the seventh moon, as anything more than the imaginings prompted by a too-lavish supper of your favourite shark's fin and peanut oil. Unless the dexterously-elusive attributes of the genial-spoken persons high in office at Pekin have deteriorated contemptibly since this one's departure, it is quite impossible for our great and enlightened Empire to be drawn into a conflict with the northern barbarians whom you indicate, against our will. When the matter becomes urgent, doubtless a prince of the Imperial line will loyally suffer himself to Pass Above, and during the period of ceremonial mourning for so pure and exalted an official it would indeed be an unseemly desecration to engage in any public business. If this failed, and an ultimatum were pressed with truly savage contempt for all that is sacred and refined, it might be well next to consider the health even of the sublime Emperor himself (or, perhaps better, that of the select and ever-present Dowager Empress); but should the barbarians still advance, and, setting the usages of civilised warfare at defiance, threaten an engagement in the midst of this unparalleled calamity, there will be no alternative but to have a formidable rebellion in the Capital. All the barbarian powers will then assemble as usual, and in the general involvement none dare move alone, and everything will have to be regarded as being put back to where it was before. It is well said, "The broken vessel can never be made whole, but it may be delicately arranged so that another shall displace it."

These barbarians, less resourceful in device, have only recently emerged from a conflict into which they do not hesitate to admit they were drawn despite their protests. Such incompetence is characteristic of their methods throughout. Not in any way disguising their purpose, they at once sent out an army of those

49

whom could be the readiest seized, certainly furnishing them with weapons, charms to use in case of emergency, and three-coloured standards (their adversaries adopting a white banner to symbolise the conciliation of their attitude, and displaying both freely in every extremity), but utterly neglecting to teach them the arts of painting their bodies with awe-inspiring forms, of imitating the cries of wild animals as they attacked, of clashing their weapons together with menacing vigour, or any of the recognised artifices by which terror may be struck into the ranks of an awaiting foeman. The result was that which the prudent must have foreseen. The more accomplished enemy, without exposing themselves to any unnecessary inconvenience, gained many advantages by their intrepid power of dissimulation—arranging their garments and positions in such a way that they had the appearance of attacking when in reality they were effecting a prudent retreat; rapidly concealing themselves among the earth on the approach of an overwhelming force; becoming openly possessed with the prophetic vision of an assured final victory whenever it could be no longer concealed that matters were becoming very desperate indeed; and gaining an effective respite when all other ways of extrication were barred against them by the stratagem of feigning that they were other than those whom they had at first appeared to be.

In the meantime the adventure was not progressing pleasantly for those chiefly concerned at home. With the earliest tidings of repulse it was discovered that in the haste of embarkation the wrong persons had been sent, all those who were really the fittest to command remaining behind, and many of these did not hesitate to write to the printed papers, resolutely admitting that they themselves were in every way better qualified to bring the expedition to a successful end, at the same time skilfully pointing out how the disasters which those in the field had incurred could easily have been avoided by acting in a precisely contrary manner.

In the emergency the most far-seeing recommended a more unbending policy of extermination. Among these, one in particular, a statesman bearing an illustrious name of two-edged import, distinguished himself by the liberal broad-mindedness of his opinions, and for the time he even did not flinch from making himself excessively unpopular by the wide and sweeping variety of his censure. "We are confessedly a barbarian nation," fearlessly declared this unprejudiced person (who, although entitled by hereditary right to carry a banner on the field of battle, with patriotic self-effacement preferred to remain at home and encourage those who were fighting by pointing out their inadequacy to the task and the extreme unlikelihood of their ever accomplishing it), "and in order to achieve our purpose speedily it is necessary to resort to the methods of barbarism." The most effective measure, as he proceeded to explain with well-thought-out detail, would be to capture all those least capable of resistance, concentrate them into a given camp, and then at an agreed signal reduce the entire assembly to what he termed, in a passage of high-minded eloquence, "a smoking hecatomb of women and children."

His advice was pointed with a crafty insight, for not only would such a course have brought the stubborn enemy to a realisation of the weakness of their position and thus paved the way to a dignified peace, but by the act itself few would have been left to hand down the tradition of a relentless antagonism. Yet with incredible obtuseness his advice was ignored and he himself was referred to at the time by those who regarded the matter from a different angle, with a scarcely-veiled dislike, which towards many of his followers took the form of building materials and other dissentient messages whenever they attempted to raise their voices publicly. As an inevitable result the conquest of the country took years, where it would have been moons had the more truly humane policy been adopted, commerce and the arts languished, and in the end so little spoil was taken that it was more common to meet six mendicants wearing the honourable embellishment of the campaign than to see one captured slave maiden offered for sale in the market places—indeed, even to this day the deficiency is clearly admitted and openly referred to as The Great "Domestic" Problem.

At various times during my residence here I have been filled with a most acute gratification when the words of those around have seemed to indicate that they recognised the undoubted superiority of the laws and institutions of our enlightened country. Sometimes, it is true, upon a more detailed investigation of the incident, it has presently appeared that either I had misunderstood the exact nature of their sentiments or they had slow-wittedly failed to grasp the precise operation of the enactment I had described; but these exceptions are clearly the outcome of their superficial training, and do not affect the fact my feeble and frequently even eccentric arguments are at length certainly moving the more intelligent into an admission of what constitutes true justice and refinement. It is not to be denied that here and there exists a prejudice against our customs even in the minds of the studious; but as this is invariably the shadow of misconception, it has frequently been my sympathetic privilege to promote harmony by means of the inexorable logic of fact and reason. "But are not your officials uncompromisingly opposed to the freedom of the Press?" said one who conversed with me on the varying phases of the two countries, and knowing that in his eyes this would constitute an unendurable offence, I at once appeased his mind. "By no means," I replied; "if anything, the exact contrary is the case. As a matter of reality, of course, there is no Press now, the all-seeing Board of Censors having wisely determined that it was not stimulating to the public welfare; but if such an institution was permitted to exist you may rest genially assured that nothing could exceed the lenient toleration which all in office would extend towards it." A similar instance of malicious inaccuracy is widely spoken of regarding our lesser ones. "Is it really a fact, Mr. Kong," exclaimed a maiden of magnanimous condescension, to this person recently, "that we poor women are despised in your country, and that among the working-classes female children are even systematically abandoned as soon as they are born?" Suffering my features to express amusement at this unending calumny, I indicated my violent contempt towards the one who had first uttered it. "So far from despising them," I continued, with ingratiating gallantry, "we recognise that they are quite necessary for the purposes of preparing our food, carrying weighty burdens, and the like; and how grotesque an action would it be for poor but affectionate parents to abandon one who in a few years' time could be sold at a really remunerative profit, this, indeed, being the principal means of sustenance in many frugal families."

On another occasion I had seated myself upon a wooden couch in one of the open spaces about the outskirts of the city, when an aged man chanced to pass by. Him I saluted with ceremonious politeness, on account of his years and the venerable dignity of his beard. Thereupon he approached near, and remarking affably that the afternoon was good (though, to use no subtle evasion, it was very evil), he congenially sat by my side and entered into familiar discourse.

"They say that in your part of the world we old grandfathers are worshipped," he said, after recounting to my ears all the most intimate details of his existence from his youth upwards; "now, might that be right?"

"Truly," I replied. "It is the unchanging foundation of our system of morality."

"Ay, ay," he admitted pleasantly. "We are a long way behind them foreigners in everything. At the rate we're going there won't be any trade nor work nor religion left in this country in another twenty years. I often wish I had gone abroad when I was younger. And if I had chanced upon your parts I should be worshipped, eh?" and at the agreeable thought the aged man laughed in his throat with simple humour.

"Assuredly," I replied; "—after you were dead."

"Eh?" exclaimed the venerable person, checking the fountain of his mirth abruptly at the word. "Dead! not before? Doesn't—doesn't that seem a bit of a waste?"

"Such has been the observance from the time of unrecorded antiquity," I replied. "'Obey parents, respect the old, loyally uphold the sovereign, and worship ancestors.'"

"Well, well," remarked the one beside me, "obedience and respect— that's something nowadays. And you make them do it?"

"Our laws are unflinching in their application," I said. "No crime is held to be more detestable than disrespect of those to whom we owe our existence."

"Quite right," he agreed, "it's a pleasure to hear it. It must be a great country, yours; a country with a future, I should say. Now, about that youngest lad of my son Henry's—the one that drops pet lizards down my neck, and threatened to put rat poison into his mother's tea when she wouldn't take him to the Military Turneyment; what would they do to him by your laws?"

"If the assertion were well sustained by competent witnesses," I replied, "it would probably be judged so execrable an offence, that a new punishment would have to be contrived. Failing that, he would certainly be wrapped round from head to foot in red-hot chains, and thus exposed to public derision."

"Ah, red-hot chains!" said the aged person, as though the words formed a pleasurable taste upon his palate. "The young beggar! Well, he'd deserve it."

"Furthermore," I continued, gratified at having found one who so intelligently appreciated the deficiencies of his own country and the unblemished perfection of ours, "his parents and immediate

53

descendants, if any should exist, would be submitted to a fate as inevitable but slightly less contemptuous—slow compression, perchance; his parents once removed (thus enclosing your venerable personality), and remoter offsprings would be merely put to the sword without further ignominy, and those of less kinship to about the fourth degree would doubtless escape with branding and a reprimand."

"Lordelpus!" exclaimed the patriarchal one, hastily leaping to the extreme limit of the wooden couch, and grasping his staff into a significant attitude of defence; "what's that for?"

"Our system of justice is all-embracing," I explained. "It is reasonably held that in such a case either that there is an inherent strain of criminality which must be eradicated at all hazard, or else that those who are responsible for the virtuous instruction of the young have been grossly neglectful of their duty. Whichever is the true cause, by this unfailing method we reach the desired end, for, as our proverb aptly says, 'Do the wise pluck the weed and leave the roots to spread?'"

"It's butchery, nothing short of Smithfield," said the ancient person definitely, rising and moving to a more remote distance as he spoke the words, yet never for a moment relaxing the aggressive angle at which he thrust out his staff before him. "You're a bloodthirsty race in my opinion, and when they get this door open in China that there's so much talk about, out you go through it, my lad, or old England will know why." With this narrow-minded imprecation on his lips he left me, not even permitting me to continue expounding what would be the most likely sentences meted out to the witnesses in the case, the dwellers of the same street, and the members of the household with whom the youth in question had contemplated forming an alliance.

Among the many contradictions which really almost seem purposely arranged to entrap the unwary in this strangely under-side-up country, is the fact that while the ennobled and those of high official rank are courteous in their attitude and urbane—frequently even to the extent of refusing money from those whom they have obliged, no matter how privately pressed upon them—the low-caste and slavish are not only deficient in obsequiousness, but are permitted to retort openly to those who address them with fitting dignity. Here such a state of things is too general to excite remark, but as instances are well called the flowers of the tree of assertion, this person will set forth the manner in which he was contumaciously opposed by an oblique-eyed outcast who attended within the stall of one selling wrought gold, jewels, and merchandise of the finer sort.

Being desirous of procuring a gift wherewith to propitiate a certain maiden's esteem, and seeing above a shop of varied attraction a suspended sign emblematic of three times repeated gild abundance I drew near, not doubting to find beneath so auspicious a token the fulfilment of an honourable accommodation. Inside the window was displayed one of the implements by which the various details of a garment are joined together upon turning a wheel, hung about with an inscription setting forth that it was esteemed at the price of two units of gold, nineteen pieces of silver, and eleven and three-quarters of the brass cash of the land, and judging that no more suitable object could be procured for the purpose, I entered the shop, and desired the attending slave to submit it to my closer scrutiny.

"Behold," I exclaimed, when I had made a feint of setting the device into motion (for it need not be concealed from you, O discreet one, that I was really inadequate to the attempt, and, indeed, narrowly escaped impaling myself upon its sudden and unexpected protrusions), "the highly-burnished surface of your dexterously arranged window gave to this engine a rich attractiveness which is altogether lacking at a closer examination. Nevertheless, this person will not recede from a perhaps too impulsive offer of one unit of gold, three pieces of silver, and four and a half brass cash," my object, of course, being that after the mutual recrimination of disparagement and over-praise we should in the length of an hour or two reach a becoming compromise in the middle distance.

"Well," responded the menial one, regarding me with an expression in which he did not even attempt to subdue the baser emotions, "you HAVE come a long way for nothing"; and he made a pretence of wishing to replace the object.

"Yet," I continued, "observe with calm impartiality how insidiously the rust has assailed the outer polish of the lacquer; perceive here upon the beneath part of wood the ineffaceable depression of a deeply-pointed blow; note well the—"

"It was good enough for you to want me to muck up out of the window, wasn't it?" demanded the obstinate barbarian, becoming passionate in his bearing rather than reluctantly, but with courteous grace, lessening the price to a trifling degree, as we regard the proper way of carrying on the enterprise.

"It is well said," I admitted, hoping that he might yet learn wisdom from my attitude of unruffled urbanity, though I feared that his angle of negotiating was unconquerably opposed to mine, "but now its many imperfections are revealed. The inelegance of its outline, the grossness of the applied colours, the unlucky combination of numbers engraved upon this plate, the—"

"Damme!" cried the utterly perverse rebel standing opposite, "why don't you keep on your Compound, you Yellow Peril? Who asked you to come into my shop to blackguard the things? Come now, who did?"

"Assuredly it is your place of commerce," I replied cheerfully, preparing to bring forward an argument, which in our country never fails to shake the most stubborn, "yet bend your eyes to the fact that at no great distance away there stands another and a more alluring stall of merchandise where—"

"Go to it then!" screamed the abandoned outcast, leaping over his counter and shouting aloud in a frenzy of uncontrollable rage. "Clear out, or I'll bend my feet—" but concluding at this point that some private calumny from which he was doubtless suffering was disturbing his mind to so great an extent that there was little likelihood of our bringing the transaction to a profitable end, I left the shop immediately but with befitting dignity.

With a fell-founded assurance that you will now be acquiring a really precise and bird's-eye-like insight into practically all phases of this country.

KONG HO.

56

LETTER VIII

Concerning the wisdom of the sublime Wei Chung and its application to the ordinary problems of existence. The meeting of three, hitherto unknown to each other, about a wayside inn, and their various manners of conducting the enterprise.

VENERATED SIRE,—You will doubtless remember the behaviour of the aged philosopher Wei Chung, when commanded by the broad-minded emperor of his time to reveal the hidden sources of his illimitable knowledge, so that all might freely acquire, and the race thereby become raised to a position of unparalleled excellence. Taking the well-disposed sovereign familiarly by the arm, Wei Chung led him to the mouth of his cave in the forest, and, standing by his side, bade him reflect with open eyes for a short space of time, and then express aloud what he had seen. "Nothing of grave import," declared the emperor when the period was accomplished; "only the trees shaken by the breeze." "It is enough," replied Wei Chung. "What, to the adroitly-balanced mind, does such a sight reveal?" "That it is certainly a windy day," exclaimed the omnipotent triumphantly, for although admittedly divine, he yet lacked the philosopher's discrimination. "On the contrary," replied the sage coldly, "that is the natural pronouncement of the rankly superficial. To the highly-trained intellect it conveys the more subtle truth that the wind affects the trees, and not the trees affect the wind. For upwards of seventy years this one has daily stood at the door of his cave for a brief period, and regularly garnering a single detail of like brilliance, has made it the well-spring for a day's reflection. As the result he now has by heart upwards of twenty-five thousand useful facts, all serviceable for original proverbs, and an encyclopaedic mind which would enable him to take a high place in a popular competition unassisted by a single work of reference." Much impressed by the adventure the charitably-inclined emperor presented Wei Chung with an onyx crown (which the philosopher at once threw into an adjacent well), and returning to his capital published a decree that each day at sunrise every person should stand at the door of his dwelling, and after observing for a period,

57

compare among themselves the details of their thoughts. By this means he hoped to achieve his imperial purpose, but although the literal part of the enactment is scrupulously maintained, especially by the slothful and defamatory, who may be seen standing at their doors and conversing together even to this day, from some unforeseen imperfection the intellectual capacity of the race has remained exactly as it was before.

Nevertheless it is not to be questioned that the system of the versatile Wei Chung was, in itself, grounded upon a far-seeing accuracy, and as the need of such a rational observation is deepened among the inconsistencies and fantastic customs of a barbarian race, I have made it a useful habit to accept as a guide for the day's behaviour the reflections engendered by the first noteworthy incident of the morning.

Upon the day with which this letter concerns itself I had set forth, in accordance with an ever-present desire, to explore some of the hidden places of the city. At the time a tempest of great ferocity was raging, and bending my head before it I had the distinction of coming into contact with a person of ill-endowed exterior at an angle where two reads met. This amiable wayfarer exchanged civilities with me after the politeness characteristic of the labouring classes towards those who differ from them in speech, dress, or colour: that is to say, he filled his pipe from my proffered store, and after lighting it threw the match into my face, and passed on with an appropriate remark.

Doubtless this insignificant occurrence would have faded without internal comment if the penetrating Wei Chung had never existed, but now, guided by his sublime precedent, I arranged the incident for the day's conduct under three reflective heads.

It was while I was meditating on the second of these that an exclamation caused me to turn, when I observed a prosperously-outlined person in the act of picking up a scrip which had the appearance of being lavishly distended with pieces of gold.

"If I had not seen you pass it, I should have opined that this hyer wallet belonged to you," remarked the justice-loving stranger (for the incident had irresistibly retarded my own footsteps), speaking the language of this land, but with an accent of penetrating harmony hitherto unknown to my ears. With these auspicious words he turned over the object upon his hand doubtfully.

"So entrancing a possibility is, as you gracefully suggest, of unavoidable denial," I replied. "Nevertheless, this person will not hesitate to join his acclamation with yours; for, as the Book of Verses wisely says, 'Even the blind, if truly polite, will extol the prospect from your house-top.'"

"That's so," admitted the one by my side. "But I don't know that there is any call for a special thanksgiving. As I happen to have more money of my own than I can reasonably spend I shall drop this in at a convenient police station. I dare say some poor critter is pining away for it now."

Pleasantly impressed by the resolute benevolence of the one who had a greater store of wealth than he could, by his own unaided efforts, dispose of, I arranged myself unobtrusively at his side, and maintaining an exhibition of my most polished and genial conversation, I sought to penetrate deeply into his esteem.

"Gaze in this direction, Kong," he said at length, calling me by name with auspicious familiarity; "I am a benighted stranger in this hyer city, and so are you, I rek'n. Suppose we liquor up, and then take a few of the side shows together."

"The suggestion is one against which I will erect no ill-disposed barrier," I at once replied, so inflexibly determined not to lose sight of a person possessing such engaging attributes as to be cheerfully prepared even to consume my rice spirit in the inverted position which his words implied if the display was persisted in. "Nevertheless," I added, with a resourceful prudence, "although by no means undistinguished among the highest literary and competitive circles of his native Yuen-ping, the one before you is incapable of walking in the footsteps of a person whose accumulations are greater than he himself can appreciably diminish."

"That's all right, Kong," exclaimed the one whom my last words fittingly described, striking the recess of his lower garment with a gesture of graceful significance. "When I take a fancy to any one it isn't a matter of dollars. I usually carry a trifle of five hundred or a thousand pounds in my pocket-book, and if we can get through that—why, there's plenty more waiting at the bank. Say, though, I hope you don't keep much about you; it isn't really safe."

"The temptation to do so is one which this person has hitherto successfully evaded," I replied. "The contents of this reptile-skin case"—and not to be outshone in mutual confidence I here displayed it openly—"do not exceed nine or ten pieces of gold and a like number of printed obligations promising to pay five pieces each."

"Put it away, Kong," he said resolutely. "You won't need that so long as you're with me. Well, now, what sort of a saloon have we here?"

As far as the opinion might be superficially expressed it had every indication of being one of noteworthy antiquity, and to the innately modest mind its unassuming diffidence might have lent an added charm. Nevertheless, on most occasions this person would have maintained an unshaken dexterity in avoiding its open door, but as the choice admittedly lay in the hands of one who carried five hundred or a thousand pieces of gold we went in together and passed through to a compartment of retiring seclusion.

In our own land, O my orthodox-minded father, where the unfailing resources of innumerable bands of dragons, spirits, vampires, ghouls, shadows, omens, and thunderstorms are daily enlisted to carry into effect the pronouncements of an appointed destiny, we have many historical examples of the inexorably converging legs of coincidence, but none, I think, more impressively arranged than the one now descending this person's brush.

We had scarcely reposed ourselves, and taken from the hands of an awaiting slave the vessels of thrice-potent liquid which in this Island is regarded as the indispensable accompaniment to every movement of existence, when a third person entered the room, and seating himself at a table some slightly removed distance away, lowered his head and abandoned himself to a display of most lavish dejection.

"That poor cuss doesn't appear to be holiday-making," remarked the sincerely-compassionate person at my side, after closely observing the other for a period; and then, moved by the overpowering munificence of his inward nature, he called aloud, "Say, stranger, you seem to have got it thickly in the neck. Is it family affliction or the whisky of the establishment?"

At these affably-intentioned words the stranger raised his eyes quickly, with an indication of not having up to that time been aware of our presence.

"Sir," he exclaimed, approaching to a spot where he could converse with a more enhanced facility, "when I loosened the restraint of an overpowering if unmanly grief, I imagined that I was alone, for I would have shunned even the most flattering sympathy, but your charitably-modulated voice invites confidence. The one before you is the most contemptible, left-handed, and disqualified outcast in creation, and he is now making his way towards the river, while his widow will be left to take in washing, his infant son to vend evening printed leaves, and his graceful and hitherto highly secluded daughters to go upon the stage."

"Say, stranger," interposed this person, by no means unwilling to engrave upon his memory this newly-acquired form of greeting, "the emotion is doubtless all-pressing, but in my ornate and flower-laden tongue we have a salutation, 'Slowly, slowly; walk slowly,' which seems to be of far-seeing application."

"That's so," remarked the one by my side. "Separate it with the teeth, inch by inch."

"I will be calm, then," continued the other (who, to avoid the complication of the intermingling circumstances, may be described as the more stranger of the two), and he took of his neckcloth. "I am a merchant in tea, yellow fat, and mixed spices, in a small but hitherto satisfactory way." Thus revealing himself, he continued to set forth how at an earlier hour he had started on a journey to deposit his wealth (doubtless as a propitiation of outraged deities) upon a certain bank, and how, upon reaching the specified point, he discovered that what he carried had eluded his vigilance. "All gone: notes, gold, and pocket-book—the savings of a lifetime," concluded the ill-omened one, and at the recollection a sudden and even more highly-sustained frenzy of self-unpopularity involving him, without a pause he addressed himself by seven and twenty insulting expressions, many of which were quite new to my understanding.

At the earliest mention of the details affecting the loss, the elbow of the person who had made himself responsible for the financial obligation of the day propelled itself against my middle part, and unseen by the other he indicated to me by means of his features that the entertainment was becoming one of agreeable prepossession.

"Now, touching this hyer wallet," he said presently. "How might you describe it?"

"In colour it was red, and within were two compartments, the one containing three score notes each of ten pounds, the other fifty pounds of gold. But what's the use of describing it? Some lucky demon will pick it up and pocket the lot, and I shall never see a cent of it again."

"Then you'd better consult one who reburnishes the eyes," declared the magnanimous one with a laugh, and drawing forth the article referred to he cast it towards the merchant in a small way.

At this point of the narrative my thoroughly incompetent brush confesses the proportions of the requirement to be beyond its most extended limit, and many very honourable details are necessarily left without expression.

"I've known men of all sorts, good, bad, and bothwise," exclaimed the one who had recovered his possessions; "but I never thought to meet a gent as would hand over six hundred and fifty pounds as if it was a toothpick. Sir, it overbalances me; it does, indeed."

"Say no more about it," urged the first person, and to suggest gracefully that the incident had reached its furthest extremity, he began to set out the melody of an unspoken verse.

"I will say no more, then," he replied; "but you cannot reasonably prevent my doing something to express my gratitude. If you are not too proud you will come and partake of food and wine with me beneath the sign of the Funereal Male Cow, and to show my confidence in you I shall insist upon you carrying my pocket-book."

The person whom I had first encountered suffered his face to become excessively amused. "Say, stranger, do you take me for a pack-mule?" he replied good-naturedly. "I already have about as much as I want to handle. Never mind; we'll come along with you, and Mr. Kong shall carry your bullion."

At this delicate and high-minded proposal a rapid change, in no way complimentary to my explicit habit of adequately conducting any venture upon which I may be engaged, came over the face of the second person.

"Sir," he exclaimed, "I have nothing to say against this gentleman, but I am under no obligation to him, and I don't see why I should trust him with everything I possess."

"Stranger," exclaimed the other rising to his feet (and from this point it must be understood that the various details succeeded one another with a really agile dexterity), "let me tell you that Mr. Kong is my friend, and that ought to be enough."

"It is. If you say this gentleman is your friend, and that you have known him long and intimately enough to be able to answer for him, that's good enough for me."

"Well," admitted the first person, and I could not conceal from myself that his tone was inauspiciously reluctant, "I can't exactly say that I've known him long; in fact I only met him half an hour ago. But I have the fullest confidence in his integrity."

"It's just as I expected. Well, sir, you're good-natured enough for anything, but if you'll excuse me, I must say that you're a small piece of an earthenware vessel after all"—the veiled allusion doubtlessly being that the vessel of necessity being broken, the contents inevitably escape—"and I hope you're not being had."

"I'm not, and I'll prove it before we go out together," retorted the engaging one, who had in the meantime become so actively impetuous on my account, that he did not remain content with the spoken words, but threw the various belongings about as he mentioned them in a really profuse display of inimitable vehemence. "Here, Kong, take this hyer pocket-book whatever he says. Now on the top of that take everything I've got, and you know what THAT figures up to. Now give this gentleman your little lot to keep him quiet; I don't ask for anything. Now, stranger, I'm ready. You and I will take a stroll round the block and back again, and if Mr. Kong isn't waiting here for us when we return with everything intact and O.K., I'll double your deposit and never trust a durned soul again."

Nodding genially over his shoulder with a harmonious understanding, expressive of the fact that we were embarking upon an undeniably diverting episode, the benevolent-souled person who had accumulated more riches than he was competent to melt away himself, passed out, urging the doubtful and still protesting one before him.

Thus abandoned to my own reflections, I pondered for a short time profitably on the third head of the day's meditation (Touching the match and this person's unattractively-lined face. The revealed truth: the inexperienced sheep cannot pass through the hedge without leaving portions of his wool), and then finding the philosophy of Wei Chung very good, I determined to remove the superfluous apprehensions of the vender of food-stuffs with less delay by setting out and meeting them on their return.

63

A few paces distant from the door, one of the ever-present watchers of the street was standing, watching the street with unremitting vigilance, while from the well-guarded expression of his face it might nevertheless be gathered that he stood as though in expectation.

"Prosperity," I said, with seasonable greeting. (For no excess of consideration is too great to be lavished upon these, who unite within themselves the courage of a high warrior, the expertness of a three-handed magician, and the courtesy of a genial mandarin.) "I seek two, apparelled thus and thus. Did you, by any chance, mark the direction of their footsteps?"

"Oh," he said, regarding this person with a most flattering application, "YOU seek them, do you? Well, they've just gone off in a hansom, and they'll want a lot of seeking for the next week or two. You let them carry your purse, perhaps?"

"Assuredly," I replied. "As a mark of confidence; this person, for his part, receiving a like token at their hands."

"That's it," said the official watcher, conveying into his voice a subtle indication that he had become excessively fatigued. "It's like a nursery tale—never too old to take with the kids. Well, come along, poor lamb, the station isn't far."

So great had become the reliance which by this time I habitually reposed in these men, that I never sought to oppose their pronouncements (such a course being not only useless but undignified), and we therefore together reached the place which the one by my side had described as a station.

From the outside the building was in no way imposing, but upon reaching an inner dungeon it at once became plain that no matter with what crime a person might be charged, even the most stubborn resistance would be unavailing. Before a fiercely-burning fire were arranged metal pincers, massive skewers, ornamental branding irons, and the usual accessories of the grill, one tool being already thrust into the heart of the flame to indicate the nature of its use, and its immediate readiness for the purpose. Pegs from which the accused could be hung by the thumbs with weights attached to the feet, covered an entire wall; chains, shackling-irons, fetters, steel rings for compressing the throat, and belts for tightening the chest, all had their appointed places, while the Chair, the Boot, the Heavy

64

Hat, and many other appliances quite unknown to our system of administering justice were scattered about.

Without pausing to select any of these, the one who led me approached a raised desk at which was seated a less warlike official, whose sympathetic appearance inspired confidence. "Kong Ho," exclaimed to himself the person who is inscribing these words, "here is an individual into whose discriminating ear it would be well to pour the exact happening without evasion. Then even if the accusation against you be that of resembling another or trafficking with unlawful Forces, he will doubtless arrange the matter so that the expiation shall be as light and inexpensive as possible."

By this time certain other officials had drawn near. "What is it?" I heard one demand, and another replied, "Brooklyn Ben and Jimmie the Butterman again. Ah, they aren't artful, are they!" but at this moment the two into whose power I had chiefly fallen having conversed together, I was commanded to advance towards them and reveal my name.

"Kong," I replied freely; and I had formed a design to explain somewhat of the many illustrious ancestors of the House, when the one at the desk, pausing to inscribe my answer in a book, spoke out.

"Kong?" he said. "Is that the christian or surname?"

"Sir-name?" replied this person between two thoughts. "Undoubtedly the one before you is entitled by public examination to the degree 'Recognised Talent,' which may, as a meritorious distinction, be held equal to your title of a warrior clad in armour. Yet, if it is so held, that would rightly be this person's official name of Paik."

"Oh, it would, would it?" said the one seated upon the high chair. "That's quite clear. Are there any other names as well?"

"Assuredly," I explained, pained inwardly that one of official rank should so slightly esteem my appearance as to judge that I was so meagrely endowed. "The milk name of Ho; Tsin upon entering the Classes; as a Great Name Cheng; another style in Quank; the official title already expressed, and T'chun, Li, Yuen and Nung as the various emergencies of life arise."

"Thank you," said the high-chair official courteously. "Now, just the name in full, please, without any velvet trimmings."

65

"Kong," began this person, desirous above all things of putting the matter competently, yet secretly perturbed as to what might be considered superfluous and what deemed a perfidious suppression, "Ho Tsin Cheng Quank—"

"Hold hard," cried this same one, restraining me with an uplifted pen. "Did you say 'Quack'?"

"Quack?" repeated this person, beginning to become involved within himself, and not grasping the detail in the right position. "In a manner of setting the expression forth—"

"Put him down, 'Quack Duck,' sir," exclaimed one of dog-like dejection who stood by. "Most of these Lascars haven't got any real names—they just go by what any one happens to call them at the time, like 'Burmese Ike' down at the Mint," and this person unfortunately chancing to smile and bow acquiescently at that moment (not with any set intention, but as a general principle of courteous urbanity), in place of his really distinguished titles he will henceforth appear among the historical records of this dynasty under what he cannot disguise from his inner misgivings to be the low-caste appellation of Quack Duck.

"Now the address, please," continued the high one, again preparing to inscribe the word, and being determined that by no mischance should this particular be offensively reported, I unhesitatingly replied, "Beneath the Sign of the Lead Tortoise, on the northern course from the Lotus Pools outside the walls of Yuen-ping."

This answer the one with the book did not immediately record. "I don't say it isn't all right when you know the parts," he remarked broad-mindedly, "but it does sound a trifle irregular. Can't you give it a number and a street?"

"I fancy it must be a pub, sir," observed another. "He said that it had a sign—the Red Tortoise."

"Well, haven't you got a London address?" said the high one, and this person being able to supply a street and a number as desired, this part of the undertaking was disposed of, to his cordial satisfaction.

"Now let me see the articles which these men left with you," commanded the chieftain of the band, and without any misleading discrepancies I at once drew forth from an inner sleeve the two scrips, of which adequate mention has already been made, another hitherto undescribed, two instruments for measuring the passing hours of the day, together with a chain of fine gold ingeniously wrought into the semblance of a cable, an ornament for the breast, set about with a jewel, two neck-cloths of a kind usually carried in the pocket, a book for recording happenings of any moment, pieces of money to the value of about eleven taels, a silver flagon, a sheathed weapon and a few lesser objects of insignificant value. These various details I laid obsequiously before the one who had commanded it, while the others stood around either in explicit silence or speaking softly beneath their breath.

"Do I understand that the two persons left all these things with you, while they took your purse in exchange?" said the high official, after examining certain obscure signs upon the metals, the contents of the third scrip, and the like.

"It cannot reasonably be denied," I replied; "inasmuch as they departed without them."

"Spontaneously?" he demanded, and in spite of the unevadible severity of his voice the expression of his nearer eye deviated somewhat.

"The spoken and conclusive word of the first was that it was his intention to commit to this one's keeping everything which he had; the assertion of the second being that with this scrip I received all that he possessed."

"While of yours, what did they get, Mr. Quack?" and the tone of the one who spoke had a much more gratifying modulation than before, while the attitudes of those who stood around had favourably changed, until they now conveyed a message of deliberate esteem.

"A serpent-skin case of two enclosures," I replied. "On the one side was a handcount of the small copper-pieces of this Island, which I had caused to be burnished and gilt for the purpose of taking back to amuse those of Yuen-ping. On the other side were two or three pages from a gravity-removing printed leaf entitled 'Bits of Tits,' with which this person weekly instructs himself in the simpler rudiments of the language. For the rest the case was controlled by a hidden spring, and inscribed about with a charm against loss, consumption by fire, or being secretly acquired by the unworthy."

"I don't think you stand in much need of that charm, Mr. Quack," remarked another of more than ordinary rank, who was also present. "Then they really got practically no money from you?"

"By no means," I admitted. "It was never literally stipulated, and whatever of wealth he possesses this person carries in a concealed spot beneath his waistbelt." (For even to these, virtuous sire, I did not deem it expedient to reveal the fact that in reality it is hidden within the sole of my left sandal.)

"I congratulate you," he said with lavish refinement. "Ben and the Butterman can be very bland and persuasive. Could you tell me, as a matter of professional curiosity, what first put you on your guard?"

"In this person's country," I replied, "there is an apt saying, 'The sagacious bird does not build his nest twice in the empty soup-toureen,' and by observing closely what has gone before one may accurately conjecture much that will follow after." It may be, that out of my insufferable shortcomings of style and expression, this answer did not convey to his mind the logical sequence of the warning; yet it would have been more difficult to show him how everything arose from the faultlessly-balanced system of the heroic Wei Chung, or the exact parallel lying between the ill-clad outcast who demanded a portion of tobacco and the cheerfully unassuming stranger who had in his possession a larger accumulation of money than he could conveniently disperse.

In such a manner I took leave of the station and those connected with it, after directing that the share of the spoil which fell by the law of this Island to my lot should be sold and the money of exchange faithfully divided among the virtuous and necessitous of both sexes. The higher officials each waved me pleasantly by the hand, according to the striking and picturesque custom of the land, while the lesser ones stood around and spoke flattering words as I departed, as "honourable," "a small piece of all-right," "astute ancient male fowl," "ah!" and the like.

With repeated assurances that however ineptly the adventure may at the time appear to be tending, as regards the essentials of true dignity and an undeviating grasp upon articles of negotiable value, nothing of a regrettable incident need be feared.

KONG HO.

LETTER IX

Concerning the proverb of the highly-accomplished horse. The various perils to be encountered in the Beneath Parts. The inexplicable journey performed by this one, and concerning the obscurity of the witchcraft employed.

VENERATED SIRE,—Among these islanders there is a proverb, "Do not place the carte" (or card, the two words having an identical purport, and both signifying the inscribed tablet of viands prepared for a banquet,) "before the horse." Doubtless the saying first arose as a timely rebuke to a certain barbarian emperor who announced his contempt for the intelligence of his subjects by conferring high mandarin rank upon a favourite steed and ceremoniously appointing it to be his chancellor; but from the narrower moral that an unreasoning animal is out of place, and even unseemly, in the entertaining hall or council chamber, the expression has in the course of time taken a wider application and is now freely used as an insidious thrust at one who may be suspected of contrariness of character, of confusing issues, or of acting in a vain or illogical manner. I had already preserved the saying among other instances of foreign thought and expression which I am collecting for your dignified amusement, as it is very characteristic of the wisdom and humour of these Outer Lands. The imagination is essentially barbaric. A horse—doubtless well-groomed, richly-caparisoned, and as intellectual as the circumstances will permit, but inevitably an animal of degraded attributes and untraceable ancestry—a horse reclining before a lavishly set-out table and considering well of what dish it shall next partake! Could anything, it appears, be more diverting! Truly to our more refined outlook the analogy is lacking both in delicacy of wit and in exactitude of balance, but to the grosser barbarian conception of what is gravity-removing it is irresistible.

I am, however, reminded of the saying by perceiving that I was on the point of recording certain details of recent occurrence without first unrolling to your mind the incidents from which it has arisen that the person who is now communicating with you is no longer reposing in the Capital, but spending a period profitably in observing the habits of those who dwell in the more secluded recesses on the outskirts of the Island. This reversal of the proper sequence of affairs would doubtless strike those around as an instance of setting the banquet before the horse. Without delay, then, to pursue the allusion to its appropriate end, I will return, as it may be said, to my nosebag.

At various points about the streets of the Capital there are certain caverns artificially let into the bowels of the earth, to which any person may betake himself upon purchasing a printed sign which he must display to the guardian of the gate. Once within the underneathmost parts he is free to be carried from place to place by means of the trains of carriages which I have already described to you, until he would return to the outer surface, when he must again display his talisman before he is permitted to pass forth. Nor is this an empty form, for upon an occasion this person himself witnessed a very bitter contention between a keeper of the barrier and one whose token had through some cause lost its potency.

In the company of the experienced I had previously gone through the trial without mischance, so that recently when I expressed a wish to visit a certain Palace, and was informed that the most convenient manner would be to descend into the nearest cavern, I had no reasonable device for avoiding the encounter. Nevertheless, enlightened sire, I will not attempt to conceal from your omniscience that I was by no means impetuous towards the adventure. Owing to the pugnacious and unworthy suspicions of those who direct their destinies, I have not yet been able to penetrate the exact connection between the movements of these hot-smoke chariots and the Unseen Forces. To a person whose chief object in life is to avoid giving offence to any of the innumerable demons which are ever on the watch to revenge themselves upon our slightest indiscretion, this uncertainty opens an unending vista of intolerable possibilities. As if to emphasise the perils of this overhanging doubt the surroundings are ingeniously arranged so as to represent as nearly as practicable the terrors of the Beneath World. Both by day and night a funereal gloom envelops the caverns, the pathways and resting-places are meagre and so constructed as to be devoid of attraction or repose, and by a skilful contrivance the natural atmosphere is secretly withdrawn and a very acrimonious sulphurous haze driven in to replace it. In sudden and unforeseen places eyes of fire open and close with disconcerting rapidity, and even change colour in vindictive significance; wooden hands are outstretched as in unrelenting rigidity against supplication, or, divining the unexpressed thoughts, inexorably

70

point, as one gazes, still deeper into the recesses of the earth; while the air is never free from the sounds of groans, shrieks, the rattling of chains, dull, hopeless noises beneath one's feet or overhead, and the hoarse wordless cries of despair with which the attending slaves of the caverns greet the distant clamour of every approaching fire-chariot. Admittedly the intention of the device is benevolently conceived, and it is strenuously asserted that many persons of corrupt habits and ill-balanced lives, upon waking unexpectedly while passing through these Beneath Parts, have abandoned the remainder of their journey, and, escaping hastily to the outer air, have from that time onwards led a pure and consistent existence; but, on the other foot, those who are compelled to use the caverns daily, freely confess that the surroundings to not in any material degree purify their lives of tranquillise the nature of their inner thoughts.

In this emergency I did not neglect to write out a diversity of charms against every possible variety of evil influence, and concealing them lavishly about my head and body, I presented myself with the outer confidence of a person who is inured to the exploit. Doubtless thereby being mistaken for one of themselves in the obscurity, I received the inscribed safeguard without opposition, and even an added sum in copper pieces, which I discreetly returned to the one behind the shutter, with the request that he would honourably burn a few joss sticks or sacrifice to a trivial amount, to the success of my journey. In such a manner I reached an awaiting train, and, taking up within it a position of retiring modesty, I definitely committed myself to the undertaking.

At the next tarrying place there entered a barbarian of high-class appearance, and being by this time less assured of my competence in the matter unaided, both on account of the multiplicity of evil omens on every side, and the perverse impulses of the guiding demon, whereby at sudden angles certain of my organs had the emotion of being left irrevocably behind and others of being snatched relentlessly forward, I approached him courteously.

"Behold," I said, "many thousand li of water, both fresh and bitter, flow between the one who is addressing you and his native town of Yuen-ping, where the tablets at the street corners are as familiar to him as the lines of his own unshapely hands; for, as it is truly said, 'Does the starling know the lotus roots, or the pomfret read its way by the signs among the upper branches of the pines?' Out of the necessities of his ignorance and your own overwhelming condescension enlighten him, therefore, whether the destination of

71

this fire-chariot by any chance corresponds with the inscribed name upon his talisman?"

Thus adjured, the stranger benevolently turned himself to the detail, and upon consulting a book of symbols he expressed himself to this wise: that after a sufficient interval I should come into a certain station, called in part after the title of the enlightened ruler of this Island, and there abandoning the train which was carrying us, I should enter another which would bring me out of the Beneath Parts and presently into the midst of that Palace which I sought. This advice seemed good, for a reasonable connection might be supposed to exist between a station so auspiciously called and a Palace bearing the harmonious name of the gracious and universally-revered sovereign-consort. Accordingly I thanked him ceremoniously, not only on my own part, but also on behalf of eleven generations of immediate ancestors, and in the name of seven generations who should come after, and he on his side agreeably replied that he was sure his grandmother would have done much for mine, and he sincerely hoped that none of his great-great-grandchildren would prove less obliging. In this intellectual manner, varied with the entertainment of profuse bows, the time passed cordially between us until the barbarian reached his own alighting stage, when he again repeated the various details of the strategy for my observance.

At this point let it be set forth deliberately that there existed no treachery in the advice, still less that this person is incapable of competently achieving the destined end of any hazard upon which he may embark when once the guiding signs have been made clear to his understanding. Whatever entanglement arose was due merely to the conflicting manners of expression used by two widely-varying races, even as our own proverb says, "What is only sauce for the cod is serious for the oyster."

At the station indicated as bearing the sign of the ruler of the country (which even a person of little discernment could have recognised by the highly-illuminated representation bearing the elusively-worded inscription, "In packets only"), I left this fire-chariot, and at once perceiving another in an attitude of departure, I entered it, as the casual barbarian had definitely instructed, and began to assure myself that I had already become expertly proficient in the art of journeying among these Beneath Regions and to foresee the time, not far distant, when others would confidently address themselves to me in their extremities. So entrancing did this contemplation grow, that this outrageous person began to compose the actual words with which he would instruct them as the occasion arose, as thus, "Undoubtedly, O virtuous and not unattractive maiden, this fire-engine will ultimately lead your refined footsteps into the street called Those who Bake Food. Do not hesitate, therefore, to occupy the vacant place by this insignificant one's side"; or, "By no means, honourable sir; the Cross of Charing is in the precisely opposite direction to that selected by this self-opinionated machine for its inopportune destination. Do not rebuke this person for his immoderate loss of mental gravity, for your mistake, though pardonable in a stranger, is really excessively diverting. Your most prudent course now will assuredly be to cast yourself from the carriage without delay and rely upon the benevolent intervention of a fire-chariot proceeding backwards."

Alas, it is truly said, "None but sword-swallowers should endeavour to swallow swords," thereby signifying the vast chasm that lies between those who are really adroit in an undertaking and those who only think that they may easily become so. Presently it began to become deeply impressed upon my discrimination that the journey was taking a more lengthy duration than I had been given to understand would be the case, while at the same time a permanent deliverance from the terrors of the Beneath Parts seemed to be insidiously lengthening out into a funereal unattainableness. The point of this person's destination, he had been assured on all hands, was a spot beyond which even the most aggressively assertive engine could not proceed, so that he had no fears of being incapably drawn into more remote places, yet when hour after hour passed and the ill-destined machine never failed in its malicious endeavours to leave each successive tarrying station, it is not to be denied that my imagination dwelt regretfully upon the true civilisation of our own enlightened country, where, by the considerate intervention of an all-wise government, the possibilities of so distressing an experience are sympathetically removed from one's path. Thus the greater part of the day had faded, and I was conjecturing that by this time we must inevitably be approaching the barren and inhospitable country which forms the northern limit of the Island, when the door suddenly opened and the barbarian stranger whom I had left many hundred li behind entered the carriage.

At this manifestation all uncertainty departed, and I now understood that to some obscure end witchcraft of a very powerful and high-caste kind was being employed around me; for in no other way was it credible to one's intelligence that a person could propel himself through the air with a speed greater than that of one of these fire-chariots, and overtake it. Doubtless it was a part of this same scheme which made it seem expedient to the stranger that he should feign a part, for he at once greeted me as though the occasion were a matter of everyday happening, exclaiming genially—

"Well, Mr. Kong, returning? And what do you think of the Palace?"

"It is fitly observed, 'To the earthworm the rice stalk is as high as the pagoda,'" I replied with adroit evasion, clearly understanding from his manner that for some reason, not yet revealed to me, a course of dissimulation was expedient in order to mislead the surrounding demons concerning my movements, and by a subtle indication of the face conveying to the stranger an assurance that I had tactfully grasped the requirement, and would endeavour to walk well upon his heels, "and therefore it would be unseemly for a person of my insignificant attainments to engage in the doubtful flattery of comparing it with the many other residences of the pure and exalted which embellish your Capital."

"Oh," said the one whom I may now suitably describe by the name of Sir Philip, "that's rather a useful proverb sometimes. Many people there?"

At this inquiry I could not disguise from myself an emotion that the person seated opposite was not diplomatically inspired in so persistently clinging to the one subject upon which he must assuredly know that I experienced an all-pervading deficiency. Nevertheless, being by this more fully convinced that the disguise was one of critical necessity, and not deeming that the essential ceremonies of one Palace would differ from those of another, no matter in what land they stood (while through all I read a clear design on Sir Philip's part that the opportunity was craftily arranged so that I might impress upon any vindictively-intentioned spirits within hearing an assumption of high protection), I replied that the gathering had been one of unparalleled splendour, both by reason of the multitude of exalted nobles present and also owing to the jewelled magnificence lavished on every detail. Furthermore, I continued, now definitely abandoning all the promptings of a wise reserve, and reflecting, as we say, that one may as well be drowned in the ocean as in a wooden bucket, not only did the sublime and unapproachable sovereign graciously permit me to kow-tow respectfully before him, but subsequently calling me to his side beneath a canopy of golden radiance, he conversed genially with me and benevolently assured me of his sympathetic favour on all occasions (this, I conjectured, would certainly overawe any Evil Force not among the very highest circles), while the no less magnanimous Prince of the Imperial Line questioned me with flattering assiduousness concerning a method of communicating with persons at a distance by means of blows or stamps upon a post (as far as the outer meaning conveyed itself to me), the houses which we build, and whether they contained an adequate provision of enclosed spaces in the walls.

Doubtless I could have continued in this praiseworthy spirit of delicate cordiality to an indefinite amount had I not chanced to observe at this point that the expression of Sir Philip's urbanity had become entangled in a variety of other emotions, not all propitious to the scheme, so that in order to retire imperceptibly within myself I smiled broad-mindedly, remarking that it was well said that the moon was only bright while the sun was hid, and that I had lately been dazzled with the sight of so much brilliance and virtuous condescension that there were occasions when I questioned inwardly how much I had really witnessed, and how much had been conveyed to me in the nature of an introspective vision.

It will already have been made plain to you, O my courtly-mannered father, that these barbarians are totally deficient in the polite art whereby two persons may carry on a flattering and highly-attuned conversation, mutually advantageous to the esteem of each, without it being necessary in any way that their statements should have more than an ornamental actuality. So wanting in this, the most concentrated form of truly well-bred entertainment, are even their high officials, that after a few more remarks, to which I made answer in a spirit of skilfully-sustained elusiveness, the utterly obtuse Sir Philip said at length, "Excuse my asking, Mr. Kong, but have you really been to the Alexandra Palace at all?"

Admittedly there are few occasions in life on which it is not possible to fail to see the inopportune or low-class by a dignified impassiveness of features, an adroitly-directed jest, or a remark of baffling inconsequence, but in the face of so distressingly straightforward a demand what can be advanced by a person of susceptible refinement when opposed to one of incomparably larger dimensions, imprisoned by his side in the recess of a fire-chariot which is leaping forward with uncurbed velocity, and surrounded by demons with whose habits and partialities he is unfamiliar?

"In a manner of expressing the circumstance," I replied, "it is not to be denied that this person's actual footsteps may have imperceptibly been drawn somewhat aside from the path of his former design. Yet inasmuch as it is truly said that the body is in all things subservient to the mind, and is led withersoever it is willed, and as your engaging directions were scrupulously observed with undeviating fidelity, it would be impertinently self-opinionated on this person's part to imply that they failed to guide him to his destination. Thus, for all ceremonial purposes, it is permissible conscientiously to assume that he HAS been there."

"I am afraid that I must not have been sufficiently clear," said Sir Philip. "Did you miss the train at King's Cross?"

"By no means," I replied firmly, pained inwardly that he should cast the shadow of such narrow incompetence upon me. "Seeing this machine on the point of setting forth on a journey, even as your overwhelming sagacity had enabled you to predict would be the case, I embarked with self-reliant confidence."

"Good lord!" murmured the person opposite, beginning to manifest an excess of emotion for which I was quite unable to account. "Then you have been in this train—your actual footsteps I mean, Mr. Kong; not your ceremonial abstract subliminal ego—ever since?"

To this I replied that his words shone like the moon at midnight with scintillating points of truth; adding, however, as the courtesies of the occasion required, that I had been so impressed with the many-sided brilliance of his conversation earlier in the day as to render the flight of time practically unnoticed by me.

"But did it never occur to you to ask at one of the stations?" he demanded, still continuing to wave his hands incapably from side to side. "Any of the porters would have told you."

"Kong Li Heng, the founder of our line, who was really great, has been dead eleven centuries, and no single fact or incident connected with his life has been preserved to influence mankind," I replied. "How much less will it matter, then, even in so limited a space of time as a hundred years, in what fashion so insignificant a person as the one before you acted on any occasion, and why, therefore, should he distress himself unnecessarily to any precise end?" In this manner I sought to place before him the dignified example of an imperturbability which can be maintained in every emergency, and at the same time to administer a plain yet scrupulously-sheathed

76

rebuke; for the inauspicious manner in which he had first drawn me on to speak confidently of the ceremonies of the Royal Palace and then held up my inadequacy to undeserved contempt had not rejoiced my imagination, and I was still uncertain how much to claim, and whether, perchance, even yet a more subtle craft lay under all.

"Well, in any case, when you go back you can claim the distinction of having been taken seven times round London, although you can't really have seen much of it," said Sir Philip. "This is a Circle train."

At this assertion I looked up. Though admittedly curved a little about the roof the chariot was in every essential degree what we should pronounce to be a square one; whereupon, feeling at length that the involvement had definitely passed to a point beyond my contemptible discernment, I spread out my hands acquiescently and affably remarked that the days were lengthening out pleasantly.

In such a manner I became acquainted with the one Sir Philip, and thereby, in a somewhat circuitous line, the original purpose which possessed my brush when I began this inept and commonplace letter is reached; for the person in question not only lay upon himself the obligation of leading me "by the strings of his apron-garment"—in the characteristic and fanciful turn of the barbarian language—to that same Palace on the following day, but thenceforth gracefully affecting to discern certain agreeable virtues in my conversation and custom of habit he frequently sought me out. More recently, on the double plea that they of his household had a desire to meet me, and that if I spent all my time within the Capital my impressions of the Island would necessarily be ill-balanced and deformed, he advanced a project that I should accompany him to a spot where, as far as I was competent to grasp the idiom, he was in the habit of sitting (doubtless in an abstruse reverie), in the country; and having assured myself by means of discreet innuendo that the seat referred to would be adequate for this person also, and that the occasion did not in any way involve a payment of money, I at once expressed my willingness towards the adventure.

With numerous expressions of unfeigned regret (from a filial point of view) that the voice of one of the maidens of the household, lifted in the nature of a defiance against this one to engage with her in a two-handed conflict of hong pong, obliges him to bring this immature composition to a hasty close.

KONG HO.

77

LETTER X

Concerning the authority of this high official, Sir Philip.
The side-slipperyness of barbarian etiquette. The hurl-
headlong sportiveness and that achieving its end by means of
curved mallets.

VENERATED SIRE,—If this person's memory is accurately poised
on the detail, he was compelled to abandon his former letter (when
on the point of describing the customs of these outer places), in
order to take part in a philosophical discussion with some of the
venerable sages of the neighbourhood.

Resuming the narration where it had reached this remote province
of the Empire, it is a suitable opportunity to explain that this same
Sir Philip is here greeted on every side with marks of deferential
submission, and is undoubtedly an official of high button, for
whenever the inclination seizes him he causes prisoners to be
sought out, and then proceeds to administer justice impartially
upon them. In the case of the wealthy and those who have face to
lose, the matter is generally arranged, to his profit and to the
satisfaction of all, by the payment of an adequate sum of money,
after the invariable custom of our own mandarincy. When this
incentive to leniency is absent it is usual to condemn the captive to
imprisonment in a cell (it is denied officially, but there is no reason
to doubt that a large earthenware vessel is occasionally used for this
purpose,) for varying periods, though it is notorious that in the case
of the very necessitous they are sometimes set freely at liberty, and
those who took them publicly reprimanded for accusing persons
from whose condition on possible profit could arise. This
confinement is seldom inflicted for a longer period than seven,
fourteen, or twenty-one days (these being lucky numbers,) except in
the case of those who have been held guilty of ensnaring certain
birds and beasts which appear to be regarded as sacred, for they
have their duly appointed attendants who wear a garb and are
trained in the dexterous use of arms, lurking with loaded weapons
in secret places to catch the unwary, both by night and day. Upheld
by the high nature of their office these persons shrink from no
encounter and even suffer themselves to be killed with resolute

unconcern; but when successful they are not denied an efficient triumph, for it is admitted that those whom they capture are marked men from that time (doubtless being branded upon the body with the name of their captor), and no future defence is availing. The third punishment, that of torture, is reserved for a class of solitary mendicants who travel from place to place, doubtless spreading the germs of an inflammatory doctrine of rebellion, for, owing to my own degraded obtuseness, the actual nature of their crimes could never be made clear to me. Of the tortures employed that known in their language as the "bath" (for which we have no real equivalent,) is the most dreaded, and this person has himself beheld men of gigantic proportions, whose bodies bore the stain of a voluntary endurance to every privation, abandon themselves to a most ignoble despair upon hearing the ill-destined word. Unquestionably the infliction is closely connected with our own ordeal of boiling water, but from other indications it is only reasonable to admit that there is an added ingredient, of which we probably have no knowledge, whereby the effect is enhanced in every degree, and the outer surface of the victim rendered more vulnerable. There is also another and milder form of torture, known as the "task", consisting either of sharp-edged stones being broken upon the body, or else the body broken upon sharp-edged stones, but precisely which is the official etiquette of the case this person's insatiable passion for accuracy and his short-sighted limitations among the more technical outlines of the language, prevent him from stating definitely.

Let it here be openly confessed that the intricately-arranged titles used among these islanders, and the widely-varying dignities which they convey, have never ceased to embarrass my greetings on all occasions, and even yet, when a more crystal insight into their strangely illogical manners enables me not only to understand them clearly myself, but also to expound their significance to others, a necessary reticence is blended with my most profuse cordiality, and my salutations to one whom I am for the first time encountering are now so irreproachably balanced, that I can imperceptibly develop them into an engaging effusion, or, without actual offence, draw back into a condition of unapproachable exclusiveness as the necessity may arise. With us, O my immaculate sire, a yellow silk umbrella has for three thousand years denoted a fixed and recognisable title. A mandarin of the sixth degree need not hesitate to mingle on terms of assured equality with other mandarins of the sixth degree, and without any guide beyond a seemly instinct he perceives the reasonableness of assuming a deferential obsequiousness before a mandarin of the fifth rank, and a counterbalancing arrogance when in the society of an official who has only risen to the seventh degree, thus conforming to that essential principle of harmonious intercourse, "Remember that Chang Chow's ceiling is Tong Wi's floor"; but who shall walk with even footsteps in a land where the most degraded may legally bear the same distinguished name as that of the enlightened sovereign himself, where the admittedly difficult but even more purposeless achievement of causing a gold mine to float is held to be more praiseworthy than to pass a competitive examination or to compose a poem of inimitable brilliance, and where one wearing gilt buttons and an emblem in his hat proves upon ingratiating approach not to be a powerful official but a covetous and illiterate slave of inferior rank? Thus, through their own narrow-minded inconsistencies, even the most ceremoniously-proficient may at times present an ill-balanced attitude. This, without reproach to himself, concerns the inward cause whereby the one who is placed to you in the relation of an affectionate and ever-resourceful son found unexpectedly that he had lost the benignant full face of a lady of exalted title.

At that time I had formed the acquaintance, in an obscure quarter of the city, of one who wore a uniform, and was addressed on all sides as the commander of a band, while the gold letters upon the neck part of his outer garment inevitably suggested that he had borne an honourable share in the recent campaign in a distant land. As I had frequently met many of similar rank drinking tea at the house of the engaging countess to whom I have alluded, I did not hesitate to prevail upon this Captain Miggs to accompany me there upon an occasion also, assuring him of equality and a sympathetic reception; but from the moment of our arrival the attitudes of those around pointed to the existence of some unpropitious barrier invisible to me, and when the one with whom I was associated took up an unassailable position upon the central table, and began to speak authoritatively upon the subject of The Virtues, the unenviable condition of the proud and affluent, and the myriads of fire-demons certainly laying in wait for those who partook of spiced tea and rich foods in the afternoon, and did not wear a uniform similar to his own, I began to recognise that the selection had been inauspiciously arranged. Upon taxing some around with the discrepancy (as there seemed to be no more dignified way of evading the responsibility), they were unable to contend against me that there were, indeed, two, if not more, distinct varieties of those bearing the rank of captain, and that they themselves belonged to an entirely different camp, wearing another dress, and possessing no authority to display the symbol of the letters S.A. upon their necks. With this admission I was content to leave the matter, in no way accusing them of actual duplicity, yet so withdrawing that any of unprejudiced standing could not fail to carry away the impression that I had been the victim of an unworthy artifice, and had been lured into their society by the pretext that they were other than what they really were.

With the bitter-flavoured memory of this, and other in no way dissimilar episodes, lingering in my throat, it need not be a matter of conjecture that for a time I greeted warily all who bore a title, a mark of rank, or any similar appendage; who wore a uniform, weapon, brass helmet, jewelled crown, coat of distinctive colour, or any excessive superfluity of pearl or metal buttons; who went forth surrounded by a retinue, sat publicly in a chair or allegorical chariot, spoke loudly in the highways and places in a tone of official pronouncement, displayed any feather, emblem, inscribed badge, or printed announcement upon a pole, or in any way conducted themselves in what we should esteem to be fitting to a position of high dignity. From this arose the absence of outward enthusiasm with which I at first received Sir Philip's extended favour; for although I had come to distrust all the reasonable signs of established power, I distrusted, to a much more enhanced degree, their complete absence; and when I observed that the one in question was never accompanied by a band of musicians or flower-strewers, that he mingled as though on terms of familiar intercourse with the ordinary passers-by in the streets, and never struck aside those who chanced to impede his progress, and that he actually preferred those of low condition to approach him on their feet, rather than in the more becoming attitude of unconditional prostration, I reasoned with myself whether indeed he could consistently be a person of well-established authority, or whether I was not being again led away from my self-satisfaction by another obliquity of barbarian logic. It was for this reason that I now welcomed the admitted power which he has of incriminating persons in a variety of punishable offences, and I perceived with an added satisfaction that here, where this privilege is more fully understood, few meet him without raising their hands to the upper part of their heads in token of unquestioning submission; or, as one would interpret the symbolism into actual words, meaning, "Thus, from this point to the underneath part of our sandals, all between lies in the hollow of your comprehensive hand."

There is a written jest among another barbarian nation that these among whom I am tarrying, being by nature a people who take their pleasures tragically, when they rise in the morning say, one to another, "Come, behold; it is raining again as usual; let us go out and kill somebody." Undoubtedly the pointed end of this adroit-witted saying may be found in the circumstance that it is, indeed, as the proverb aptly claims, raining on practically every occasion in life; while, to complete the comparison, for many dynasties past this nation has been successfully engaged in killing people (in order to promote their ultimate benefit through a momentary inconvenience,) in every part of the world. Thus the lines of parallel thought maintain a harmonious balance beyond the general analogy of their sayings; but beneath this may be found an even subtler edge, for in order to inure themselves to the requirement of a high destiny their various games and manners of disportment are, with a set purpose, so rigorously contested that in their progress most of the weak and inefficient are opportunely exterminated.

There is a favourite and well-attended display wherein two opposing bands, each clad in robes of a distinctive colour, stand in extended lines of mutual defiance, and at a signal impetuously engage. The design of each is by force or guile to draw their opponents into an unfavourable position before an arch of upright posts, and then surging irresistibly forward, to carry them beyond the limit and hurl them to the ground. Those who successfully inflict this humiliation upon their adversaries until they are incapable of further resistance are hailed victorious, and sinking into a graceful attitude receive each a golden cup from the magnanimous hands of a maiden chose to the service, either on account of her peerless outline, the dignified position of her House, or (should these incentives be obviously wanting,) because the chief ones of her family are in the habit of contributing unstintingly to the equipment of the triumphal band. There is also another kind of strife, differing in its essentials only so far that all who engage therein are provided with a curved staff, with which they may dexterously draw their antagonists beyond the limits, or, should they fail to defend themselves adequately, break the smaller bones of their ankles. But this form of encounter, despite the use of these weapons, is really less fatal than the other, for it is not a permissible act to club an antagonist resentfully about the head with the staff, nor yet even to thrust it rigidly against his middle body. From this moderation the public countenance extended to the curved-pole game is contemptibly meagre when viewed by the side of the overwhelming multitudes which pour along every channel in order to witness a more than usually desperate trial of the hurl-headlong variety (the sight, indeed, being as attractive to these pale, blood-thirsty foreigners as an unusually

82

large execution is with us), and as a consequence the former is little reputed save among maidens, the feeble, and those of timorous instincts.

Thus positioned, regarding a knowledge of their outside amusements, it has always been one of the most prominent ambitions of this person's strategy to avoid being drawn into any encounter. At the same time, the thought that the maidens of the household here (of whom there are several, all so attractively proportioned that to compare them in a spirit of definite preference would be distastefully presumptuous to this person,) should regard me as one lacking in a sufficient display of violence was not fragrant to my sense of refinement; so that when Sir Philip, a little time after our arrival, related to me that on the following day he and a chosen band were to be engaged in the match of a cricket game against adversaries from the village, and asked whether I cared to bear a part in the strife, I grasped the muscles of the upper part of my left arm with my right hand—as I had frequently seen the hardy and virile do when the subject of their powers had been raised questioningly—and replied that I had long concealed an insatiable wish to take such a part at a point where the conflict would be the most revengefully contested.

Being thus inflexibly committed it became very necessary to arrange a well-timed intervention (whether in the nature of bodily disorder, fire, or demoniacal upheaval, a warning omen, or the death of some of our chief antagonists), but before doing so I was desirous of understanding how this contest, which had hitherto remained outside my experience, was waged.

There is here one of benevolent rotundity in whose authority lie the cavernous stores beneath the house and the vessels of gold and silver; of menial rank admittedly, yet exacting a seemly deference from all by the rich urbanity of his voice and the dignity of his massive proportions. In the affable condescension of his tone, and the discriminating encouragement of his attitude towards me on all occasions, I have read a sympathetic concern over my welfare. Him I now approached, and taking him aside, I first questioned him flatteringly about his age and the extent of his yearly recompense, and then casually inquired what in his language he would describe the nature of a cricket to be.

"A cricket?" repeated the obliging person readily; "a cricket, sir, is a hinsect. Something, I take it, after the manner of a grass-'opper."

"Truly," I agreed. "It is aptly likened. And, to continue the simile, a game cricket—?"

"A game cricket?" he replied; "well, sir, naturally a game one would be more gamier than the others, wouldn't it?"

"The inference is unflinching," I admitted, and after successfully luring away his mind from any significance in the inquiry by asking him whether the gift of a lacquered coffin or an embroidered shroud would be the more regarded on parting, I left him.

His words, esteemed, for a definite reason were as the jade-clappered melody of a silver bell. This trial of sportiveness, it became clear,—less of a massacre than most of their amusements— is really a rivalry of leapings and dexterity of the feet: a conflict of game crickets or grass-hoppers, in the somewhat wide-angled obscurity of their language, or, as we would more appropriately call it doubtless, a festive competition in the similitude of high-spirited locusts. To whatever degree the surrounding conditions might vary, there could no longer be a doubt that the power of leaping high into the air was the essential constituent of success in this barbarian match of crickets—and in such an accomplishment this person excelled from the time of his youth with a truly incredible proficiency. Can it be a reproach, then, that when I considered this, and saw in a vision the contempt of inferiority which I should certainly be able to inflict upon these native crickets before the eyes of their maidens, even the accumulated impassiveness of thirty-seven generations of Kong fore-fathers broke down for the moment, and unable to restrain every vestige of emotion I crept unperceived to the ancestral hall of Sir Philip and there shook hands affectionately with myself before each of the nine ironclad warriors about its walls before I could revert to a becoming state of trustworthy unconcern. That night in my own upper chamber I spent many hours in testing my powers and studying more remarkable attitudes of locust flight, and I even found to be within myself some new attainments of life-like agility, such as feigning the continuous note of defiance with which the insect meets his adversary, as remaining poised in the air for an appreciable moment at the summit of each leap, and of conveying to the body a sudden and disconcerting sideway movement in the course of its ascent. So immersed did I become in the achievement of a high perfection that, to my never-ending self-reproach, I failed to notice a supernatural visitation of undoubted authenticity; for the next morning it was widely admitted that a certain familiar demon of the house, which only manifests its presence on occasions of tragic omen, had been heard throughout the night in warning, not only beating its head and body against the walls and doors in despair, but raising from time to time a wailing cry of soul-benumbing bitterness.

With every assurance that the next letter, though equally distorted in style and immature in expression, will contain the record of a deteriorated but ever upward-striving son's ultimate triumph.

KONG HO.

LETTER XI

Concerning the game which we should call "Locusts," and the deeper significance of its acts. The solicitous warning of one passing inwards and the complication occasioned by his ill-chosen words. Concerning that victory already dimly foreshadowed.

VENERATED SIRE,—This barbarian game of agile grass-hoppers is not conducted in the best spirit of a really well-balanced display, and although the one now inscribing his emotions certainly achieved a wide popularity, and wore his fig leaves with becoming modesty, he has never since been quite free from an overhanging doubt that the compliments and genial remarks with which he was assailed owed their modulation to an unsubstantial atmosphere of two-edged significance which for a period enveloped all whom he approached; as in the faces of maidens concealed behind fans when he passed, the down-drawn lips and up-raised eyes of those of fuller maturity, the practice in most of his own kind of turning aside, pressing their hands about their middle parts, and bending forward into a swollen attitude devoid of grace, on the spur of a sudden remembrance, and in the auspicious but undeniably embarrassing manner in which all the unfledged ones of the village clustered about his retiring footsteps, saluting him continually as one "James," upon whom had been conferred the gratifying title of "Sunny." Thus may the outline of the combat be recounted.

From each opposing group eleven were chosen as a band, and we of our company putting on a robe of distinctive green (while they elected to be regarded as an assemblage of brown crickets), we presently came to a suitable spot where the trial was to be decided. So far this person had reasonably assumed that at a preconcerted signal the contest would begin, all rising into the air together, uttering cries of menace, bounding unceasingly and in every way displaying the dexterity of our proportions. Indeed, in the reasonableness of this expectation it cannot be a matter for reproach to one of the green grass-hoppers—who need not be further indicated—that he had already begun a well-simulated note of challenge to those around clad in brown, and to leap upwards in a preparatory essay, when the ever-alert Sir Philip took him affectionately by the arm, on the plea that the seclusion of a neighbouring pavilion afforded a desirable shade.

Beyond that point it is difficult to convey an accurately grouped and fully spread-out design of the encounter. In itself the scheme and intention of counterfeiting the domestic life and rivalries of two opposing bands of insects was pleasantly conceived, and might have been carried out with harmonious precision, but, after the manner of these remote tribes, the original project had been overshadowed and the purity of the imagination lost beneath a mass of inconsistent detail. To this imperfection must it be laid that when at length this person was recalled from the obscurity of the pagoda and the alluring society of a maiden of the village, to whom he was endeavouring to expound the strategy of the game, and called upon to engage actively in it, he courteously admitted to those who led him forth that he had not the most shadowy-outlined idea of what was required of him.

Nevertheless they bound about his legs a frilled armour, ingeniously fashioned to represent the ribbed leanness of the insect's shank, encased his hands and feet in covers to a like purpose, and pressing upon him a wooden club indicated that the time had come for him to prove his merit by venturing alone into the midst of the eleven brown adversaries who stood at a distance in poised and expectant attitudes.

Assuredly, benignant one, this sport of contending locusts began, as one approached nearer to it, to wear no more pacific a face than if it had been a carnage of the hurl-headlong or the curved-hook varieties. In such a competition, it occurred to him, how little deference would be paid to this one's title of "Established Genius," or how inadequately would he be protected by his undoubted capacity of leaping upwards, and even in a sideway direction, for no matter how vigorously he might propel himself, or how successfully he might endeavour to remain self-sustained in the air, the ill-destined moment could not be long deferred when he must come down again into the midst of the eleven—all doubtless concealing weapons as massive and fatally-destructive as his own. This prospect, to a person of quiescent taste, whose chief delight lay in contemplating the philosophical subtleties of the higher Classics, was in itself devoid of glamour, but with what funereal pigments shall he describe his sinking emotions when one of his own band, approaching him as he went, whispered in his ear, "Look out at this end; they kick up like the very devil. And their man behind the wicket is really smart; if you give him half a chance he'll have your stumps down before you can say 'knife.'" Shorn of its uncouth familiarity, this was a charitable warning that they into whose stronghold I was turning my footsteps—perhaps first deceiving my alertness with a proffered friendship—would kick with the ferocity of untamed demons, and that one in particular, whose description, to my added despair, I was unable to retain, was known to possess a formidable knife, with which it was his intention to cut off this person's legs at the first opportunity, before he could be accused of the act. Truly, "To one whom he would utterly destroy Buddha sends a lucky dream."

Behind lay the pagoda (though the fact that this one did admittedly turn round for a period need not be too critically dwelt upon), with three tiers of maidens, some already waving their hands as an encouraging token; on each side a barrier of prickly growth inopportunely presented itself, while in front the eleven kicking crickets stood waiting, and among them lurked the one grasping a doubly-edged blade of a highly proficient keenness.

There are occasional moments in the life of a person when he as the inward perception of retiring for a few paces and looking back in order to consider his general appearance and to judge how he is situated with regard to himself, to review his past life in a spirit of judicial severity, to arrange definitely upon a future composed entirely of acts of benevolence, and to examine the working of destiny at large. In such a scrutiny I now began to understand that it would perhaps have been more harmonious to my love of contemplative repose if I had considered the disadvantages closer before venturing into this barbarian region, or, at least, if I had used the occasion profitably to advance an argument tending towards a somewhat fuller allowance of taels from your benevolent sleeve. Our own virtuous and flower-strewn land, it is true, does not possess an immunity from every trifling drawback. The Hoang Ho—to concede specifically the existence of some of these—frequently bursts through its restraining barriers and indiscriminately sweeps away all those who are so ill-advised as to dwell within reach of its malignant influence. From time to time wars and insurrections are found to be necessary, and no matter how morally-intentioned and humanely conducted, they necessarily result in the violation, dismemberment or extirpation of many thousand polite and dispassionate persons who have no concern with either side. Towns are repeatedly consumed by fire, districts scourged by leprosy, and

88

provinces swept by famine. The storms are admittedly more fatal than elsewhere, the thunderbolts larger, more numerous, and all unerringly directed, while the extremities of heat and cold render life really uncongenial for the greater part of each year. The poor, having no money to secure justice, are evilly used, whereas the wealthy, having too much, are assailed legally by the gross and powerful for the purpose of extorting their riches. Robbers and assassins lurk in every cave; vast hoards of pirates blacken the surface of every river; and mandarins of the nine degrees must make a livelihood by some means or other. By day, therefore, it is inadvisable to go forth and encounter human beings, while none but the shallow-headed would risk a meeting with the countless demons and vampires which move by night. To one who has spent many moons among these foreign apparitions the absence of drains, roads, illustrated message-parchments, maidens whose voices may be heard protesting upon ringing a wire, loaves of conflicting dimensions, persons who strive to put their faces upon every advertisement, pens which emit fountains when carried in the pocket, a profusion of make-strong foods, and an Encyclopaedia Mongolia, may undoubtedly be mentioned as constituting a material deficiency. Affairs are not being altogether reputably conducted during the crisis; it can never be quite definitely asserted what the next action of the versatile and high-spirited Dowager Empress will be; and here it is freely contended that the Pure and Immortal Empire is incapable of remaining in one piece for much longer. These, and other inconveniences of a like nature, which the fastidious might distort into actual hardships, have never been denied, yet at no period of the nine thousand years of our civilisation has it been the custom to lure out the unwary, on the plea of an agreeable entertainment, and then to abandon him into the society of eleven club-bearing adversaries, one of whom may be depicted as in the act of imparting an unnecessary polish to the edge of his already preternaturally acute weapon, while those of his own band offer no protection, and three tiers of very richly-dressed maidens encourage him to his fate by refined gestures of approval.

Doubtless this person had unconsciously allowed his inner meditations to carry him away, as it may be expressed, for when he emerged from this strain of reverie it was to discover himself in the chariot-road and—so incongruously may be the actions when the controlling intelligence is withdrawn—even proceeding at a somewhat undignified pace in a direction immediately opposed to an encounter with the brown locusts. From this mortifying position he was happily saved by emerging from these thought-dreams before it was too late to return, and, also, if the detail is not too insignificant to be related, by the fact that certain chosen runners from his own company had reached a point in the road before him, and now stood joining their outstretched arms across the passage and raising gravity-dispelling cries. Smiling acquiescently, therefore, this person returned in their midst, and receiving a new weapon, his own club having been absent-mindedly mislaid, he again set forth warily to the encounter.

Yet in this he did not altogether neglect a discreet prudence. The sympathetic person to whom he was indebted for the pointed allusion had specifically declared that they who used their feet with the desperate savagery of baffled spectres guarded the nearer limits of their position, the intention of his timely hint assuredly being that I should seek to approach from the opposite end, where, doubtless, the more humane and conciliatory grass-hoppers were assembled. Thus guided I now set forth in a widely-circuitous direction, having the point where I meant to open an attack clearly before my eyes, yet seeking to deliver a more effective onslaught by reaching it to some extent unperceived and to this end creeping forward in the protecting shadow of the long grass and untrimmed herbage.

Whether the one already referred to had incapably failed to express his real meaning, or whether he was tremulous by nature and inordinately self-deficient, concerns the narration less than the fact that he had admittedly produced a state of things largely in excess of the actual. There is no longer any serviceable pretext for maintaining that those guarding any point of their position were other than mild and benevolent, while the only edged weapon displayed was one courteously produced to aid this person's ineffectual struggles to extricate himself when, by some obscure movement, he had most ignobly entangled his pigtail about the claws of his sandal.

Ignorant of this, the true state of things, I was still advancing subtly when one wearing the emblems of our band appeared from among the brown insects and came towards me. "Courage!" I exclaimed in a guarded tone, raising my head cautiously and rejoiced to find that I should not be alone. "Here is one clad in green bearing succour, who will, moreover, obstinately defend his stumps to the last extremity."

"That's right," replied the opportune person agreeably; "we need a few like that. But do get up on your hind legs and come along,

90

there's a good fellow. You can play at bears in the nursery when we get back, if you want."

Certainly one can simulate the movements of wild animals in a market-garden if the impersonation is thought to be desirable, yet the reasonable analogy of the saying is elusive in the extreme, and I followed the ally who had thus betrayed my presence with a deep-set misgiving although in the absence of a more trustworthy guide, and in the suspicion that some point of my every ordinary strategy had been inept, I was compelled to mould myself identically into his advice.

Scarcely had he left me, and I was endeavouring to dispel any idea of treachery towards those about by actions of graceful courtesy, when one—unworthy of burial—standing a score of paces distant, (to whom, indeed, this person was at the moment bowing with almost passionate vehemence, inspired by the conviction that he, for his part, was engaged in a like attention,) suddenly cast a missile—which, somewhat double-facedly, he had hitherto held concealed in his closed hand—with undeviating force and accuracy. So unexpected was the movement, so painfully-impressed the vindictive contact, that I should have instinctively seized the offensively-directed object and contemptuously hurled it back again, if the consequence of the blow had not deprived my mind of all retaliatory ambitions. In this emergency was manifested a magnanimous act worthy of the incense of a poem, for a person standing immediately by, seeing how this one was balanced in his emotions, picked up the missile, and although one of the foremost of the opposing band, very obligingly flung it back at the assailant. Even an outcast would not have passed this without a suitable tribute, and turning to him, I was remarking appreciatively that men were not divided by seas and wooden barriers, but by the unchecked and conflicting lusts of the mind, when the unclean and weed-nurtured traitor twenty paces distant, taking a degraded advantage from this person's attitude, again propelled his weapon with an even more concentrated perfidy than before. At this new outrage every brown cricket shrank from the attitude of alert vigour which hitherto he had maintained, and as though to disassociate themselves from the stain of complicity all crossed over and took up new positions.

Up to this point, majestic head, in order to represent the adventure in its proper sequence, it has been advisable to present the details as they arose before the eyes of a reliable and dispassionate gazer.

91

Now, however, it is no less seemly to declare that this barbarian sport of leaping insects is not so discreditably shallow as it had at first appeared, while in every action there may be found an apt but hidden symbol. Thus the presence of the two green locusts in the midst of others of a dissimilar nature represents the unending strife by which even the most pacific are ever surrounded. The fragile erection of sticks (behind which this person at first sought to defend himself until led into a more exposed position by one garbed in white,) may be regarded as the home and altar, and adequately depicts the hollowness of the protection it affords and the necessity of reliantly emerging to defy an invader rather than lurking discreditably among its recesses. The missile is the equivalent of a precise and immediate danger, the wooden club the natural instinct for defence with which all living creatures are endowed, so that when the peril is for the time driven away the opportunity is at hand for the display of virtuous amusements, the exchanging of hospitality, and the beating of professional drums as we would say. Thus, at the next attack the one sharing the enterprise with me struck the missile so proficiently that its recovery engaged the attention of all our adversaries, and then began to exhibit his powers by running and leaping towards me. Recognising that the actual moment of the display had arrived, this person at once emitted a penetrating cry of concentrated challenge, and also began to leap upwards and about, and with so much energy that the highly achieved limits of his flight surprised even himself.

As for the bystanders, esteemed, those who opposed us, and the members of our own band, although this leaping sportiveness is a competition more regarded and practised among all orders than the pursuit of commercial eminence, or even than the allurements of the sublimest Classics, it may be truly imagined that never before had they witnessed so remarkable a game cricket. From the pagoda a loud cry of wonder acclaimed the dexterity of this person's efforts; the three tiers of maidens climbed one upon another in their anxiety to lose no detail of the adventure, and outstanders from distant points began to assemble. The brown enemy at once abandoned themselves to a panic, and for the most part cast themselves incapably to the ground, rolling from side to side in an access of emotion; the two arbiters clad in white conferred together, doubtless on the uselessness of further contest, while the ally who had summoned me to take a part instead of being encouraged to display his agility in a like manner continued to run slavishly from point to point, while I overcame the distances in a series of inspired bounds.

In the meanwhile the sounds of encouragement from the ever-increasing multitude grew like the falling of a sudden coast storm among the ripe leaves of a tea-plantation, and with them the voices of many calling upon my name and inciting me to further and even higher achievements reached my ears. Not to grow small in the eyes of these estimable persons I continued in my flight, and abandoning all set movements and limits, I began to traverse the field in every direction, becoming more proficient with each effort, imparting to myself a sideway and even backward motion while yet in the upper spaces, remaining poised for an appreciable period, and lightly, yet with graceful ease, avoiding the embraces of those who would have detained me. Undoubtedly I could have maintained this supremacy until our band might justly have claimed the reward, had not the flattering cries of approval caused an indiscreet mistake, for the alarm being spread in the village that a conflagration of imposing ferocity was raging, an ornamental chariot conveying a band of warriors clad in brass armour presently entered into the strife, and discovering no fire to occupy their charitable energies they misguidedly honoured this offensive person by propelling a solid column of the purest and most refreshing water against his ignoble body when at the point of his highest flight. This introduction of a thunderbolt into the everyday life of an insect must be of questionable authenticity, yet not feeling sufficiently instructed in the lesser details of the sportiveness to challenge the device, I suffered myself to be led towards the pavilion with no more struggling than enough to remove the ignominy of an unresisting surrender, pleasantly remarking to those who bore me along that to a person of philosophical poise the written destiny was as apparent in the falling leaf as in the rising sun, pointing the saying thus: "Although the Desert of Shan-tz is boundless, and mankind number a million million, yet in it Li-hing encountered his mother-in-law." Changing to meet another of our company setting forth with a club to make the venture, I was permitted for a moment to engage him; whereupon thrusting into his hand a leather charm against ill-directed efforts, and instructing him to bind it about his head, I encouraged him with the imperishable watch-word of the Emperor Tsin Su, "The stars are indeed small, but their light carries as far as that of the full moon."

At the steps of the pagoda so great was the throng of those who would have overwhelmed me with their gracious attention, that had not this person's neck become practically automatic by ceaseless use of late, he would have been utterly unequal to the emergency. As it was, he could only bestow a superficial hand-wave upon a company

93

of gold-embroidered musicians who greeted his return with appropriate melody, and a glance of well-indicated regret that he had no fuller means of conveying his complicated emotions, in the direction of the uppermost tier of maidens. Then the awaiting Sir Philip took him firmly towards the inner part of the pavilion, and announced, so adroitly and with such high-spirited vigour had this one maintained the conflict, that it had been resolutely agreed on all sides not to make a test of his competence any further.

Thereupon a band of very sumptuously arrayed nymphs drew near with offerings of liquid fat and a variety of crimson fruit, which it is customary to grind together on the platter—unapproachable in the result, certainly, yet incredibly elusive to the unwary in the manner of bruising, and practically ineradicable upon the more delicate shades of silk garment. In such a situation the one who is now relating the various incidents of the day may be imagined by a broad-minded and affectionate sire: partaking of this native fruit and oil, and from time to time expressing his insatiable anguish that he continually fails to become more proficient in controlling the oblique movements of the viands, while the less successful crickets are constrained to persevere in the combat, and the ever-present note of evasive purport is raised by a voice from behind a screen exclaiming, "Out afore? That he may have been, but do he think we was a-going to give he out afore? No, maaster, us doant a-have a circus every day hereabouts."

Thus may this imagination of competitive locusts be set forth to the end. If a fuller proof of what an unostentatious self-effacement hesitates to enlarge upon were required, it might be found in the barbarian printed leaf, for the next day this person saw a public record of the strife, in which his own name was followed by a numerical emblem signifying that he had not stumbled or proved incompetent in any one particular. Sir Philip, I beheld with pained surprise, had obtusely suffered himself to be caught out in the committal of fifty-nine set offences.

With a not unnatural anticipation that, as a result of this painstaking description, this person will find two well-equipped camps of contending locusts in Yuen-ping on his return.

KONG HO.

94

Concerning the obvious misunderstanding which has entwined itself about a revered parent's faculties of passionless discrimination. The all-water disportment and the two, of different sexes, who after regarding me conflictingly from the beginning, ended in a like but inverted manner.

VENERATED SIRE,—Your gem-adorned letter containing a thousand burnished words of profuse reproach has entered my diminished soul in the form of an equal number of rusty barbs. Can it be that the incapable person whom, as you truly say, you sent, "to observe the philosophical subtleties of the barbarians, to study their dynastical records and to associate liberally with the venerable and dignified," has, in your own unapproachable felicity of ceremonial expression, "according to a discreet whisper from many sources, chiefly affected the society of tea-house maidens, the immature of both sexes, doubtful characters of all classes, and criminals awaiting trial; has evinced an unswerving affinity towards light amusement and entertainments of a no-class kind; and in place of a wise aloofness, befitting a wearer of the third Gold Button and the Horn Belt-clasp, in situations of critical perplexity, seems by his own ingenuous showing to have maintained an unparalleled aptitude for behaving either with the crystalline simplicity of a Kan-su earth-tiller, or the misplaced buffoonery of a seventh-grade body-writher taking the least significant part in an ill-equipped Swatow one-cash Hall of Varied Melodies." Assuredly, if your striking and well-chosen metaphors were not more unbalanced than the ungainly attitude of a one-legged hunchback crossing a raging torrent by means of a slippery plank on a stormy night, they would cause the very acutest bitterness to the throat of a dutiful and always high-stepping son. There is an apt saying, however, "A quarrel between two soldiers in the market-place becomes a rebellion in the outskirts," and when this person remembers that many thousand li of mixed elements flow between him and his usually correct and dispassionate sire, he is impelled to take a mild and tolerant attitude towards the momentary injustice brought about by the weakness of approaching old age, the vile-intentioned mendacity of outcasts envious of the House of Kong, and, perchance, the irritation brought on by a too lavish indulgence in your favourite dish of stewed mouse.

Having thus re-established himself in the clear-sighted affection of an ever mild and perfect father, and cleansed the ground of all possible misunderstandings in the future, this person will concede the fact that, not to stand beneath the faintest shadow of an implied blemish in your sympathetic eyes, he had no sooner understood the attitude in which he had been presented than he at once plunged into the virtuous society of a band of the sombre and benevolent.

These, so far as his intelligence enables him to grasp the position, may be reasonably accepted as the barbarian equivalent of those very high-minded persons who in our land devote their whole lives secretly to killing others whom they consider the chief deities do not really approve of; for although they are not permitted here, either by written law or by accepted custom, to perform these meritorious actions, they are so intimately initiated into the minds and councils of the Upper Ones that they are able to pronounce very severe judgments of torture—a much heavier penalty than merely being assassinated—upon all who remain outside their league. As some of the most objurgatory of these alliances do not number more than a score of persons, it is inevitable that the ultimate condition of the whole barbarian people must be hazardous in the extreme.

Having associated myself with this class sufficiently to escape their vindictive pronouncements, and freely professed an unswerving adherence to their rites, I next sought out the priests of other altars, intending by a seemly avowal to each in turn to safeguard my future existence effectually. This I soon discovered to be beyond the capacity of an ordinary lifetime, for whereas we, with four hundred million subjects find three religions to be sufficient to meet every emergency, these irresolute island children, although numbering us only as one to ten, vacillate among three hundred; and even amid this profusion it is asserted that most of the barbarians are unable to find any temple exactly conforming to their requirements, and after writing to the paper to announce the fact, abandon the search in despair.

It was while I was becoming proficient in the inner subtleties of one of these orders—they who drink water on all occasions and wear a badge—that a maiden of some authority among them besought my aid for the purpose of amusing a band which she was desirous of

96

propitiating into the adoption of this badge. It is possible that in the immature confidence of former letters this person may already have alluded to certain maidens with words of courteous esteem, but it is now necessary to admit finally that in the presence of this same Helena they would all appear as an uninviting growth of stunted and deformed poppies surrounding a luxuriant chrysanthemum. At the presumptuous thought of describing her illimitable excellences my fingers become claw-like in their confessed inadequacy to hold a sufficiently upright brush; yet without undue confidence it may be set down that her hands resembled the two wings of a mandarin drake in their symmetrical and changing motion, her hair as light and radiant-pointed as the translucent incense cloud floating before the golden Buddha of Shan-Si, thin white satin stretched tightly upon polished agate only faintly comparable to her jade cheeks, while her eyes were more unfathomable than the crystal waters of the Keng-kiang, and within their depths her pure and magnanimous thoughts could be dimly seen to glide like the gold and silver carp beneath the sacred river.

When this insurpassable being approached me with the flattering petition already alluded to, my gratified emotions clashed together uncontrollably with the internal feeling of many volcanoes in movement, and my organs of expression became so entangled at the condescension of her melodious voice being directly addressed to one so degraded, that for several minutes I was incapable of further acquiescence than that conveyed by an adoring silence and an unchanging smile. No formality appeared worthy to greet her by, no expression of self-contempt sufficiently offensive to convey to her enlightenment my own sense of a manifold inferiority, and doubtless I should have remained in a transfixed attitude until she had at length turned aside, had not your seasonable reference to a Swatow limb-contorter struck me heavily and abruptly turned off the source of my agreement. Might not this all-water entertainment, it occurred to this one, consist in enticing him to drink a potion made unsuspectedly hot, in projecting him backwards into a vat of the same liquid, or some similar device for the pleasurable amusement of those around, which would come within the boundaries of your refined disapproval? As one by himself there was no indignity that this person would not cheerfully have submitted to, but the inexorable cords of an ingrained filial regard suddenly pulled him sideways and into another direction.

"But, Mr. Kong," exclaimed the bee-lipped maiden, when I had explained (as being less involved to her imagination,) that I was under a vow, "we have been relying upon you. Could you not"—and here she dropped her eyes and picked them up again with a fluttering motion which our lesser ones are, to an all-wise end, quite unacquainted with—"could you not unvow yourself for one night, just to please ME?"

At these words, the illuminated proficiency of her glance, and her honourable resolution to implicate me in the display by head or feet, the ever-revered image of a just and obedience-loving father ceased to have any further tangible influence. Let it be remembered that there is a deep saying, "A virtuous woman will cause more evil than ten river pirates." As for the person who is recording his incompetence, the room and all those about began to engulf him in an ever-increasing circular motion, his knees vibrated together with unrestrained pliancy, and concentrating his voice to indicate by the allegory some faint measure of his emotion, he replied passionately, "Let the amusement referred to take the form of sitting in a boiling cauldron exposed to the derision of all beholders, this one will now enter it wearing yellow silk trousers."

It is characteristic of these illogical out-countries that the all-water diversion did not, as a matter to record, concern itself with that liquid in any detail, beyond the contents of a glass vessel from which a venerable person, who occupied a raised chair, continually partook. This discriminating individual spoke so confidently of the beneficial action of the fluid, and so unswervingly described my own feelings at the moment—as of head giddiness, an inexactitude of speech, and no clear definition of where the next step would be arrived at—as the common lot of all who did not consume regularly, that when that same Helena had passed on to speak to another, I left the hall unobserved and drank successive portions, in each case, as the night was cold, prudently adding a measure of the native rice spirit. His advice had been well-directed, for with the fourth portion I suddenly found all doubtful and oppressive visions withdrawn, and a new and exhilarating self-confidence raised in their place. In this agreeable temper I returned to the place of meeting to find a priest of one of the lesser orders relating a circumstance whereby he had encountered a wild maiden in the woods, who had steadfastly persisted that she was one of a band of seven (this being the luckiest protective number among the superstitious). Though unable to cause their appearance, she had gone through a most precise examination at his hands without deviating in the slightest particular, whereupon distrusting the outcome of the strife, the person who was relating the adventure had withdrawn breathless.

When this versatile lesser priest had finished the narration, and the applause, which clearly showed that those present approved of the solitary maiden's discreet stratagem, had ceased, the one who occupied the central platform, rising, exclaimed loudly, "Mr. Kong will next favour us with a contribution, which will consist, I am informed, of a Chinese tale."

Now there chanced to be present a certain one who had already become offensive to me by the systematic dexterity with which he had planted his inopportune shadow between the sublime-souled Helena and any other who made a movement to approach her heaven-dowered outline. When this presumptuous and ill-nurtured outcast, who was, indeed, then seated by the side of the enchanting maiden last referred to, heard the announcement he said in a voice feigned to reach her peach-skin ear alone, yet intentionally so modulated as to penetrate the furthest limit of the room, "A Chinese tale! Why, assuredly, that must be a pig-tail." At this unseemly shaft many of those present allowed themselves to become immoderately amused, and even the goat-like sage who had called upon my name concealed his face behind an open hand, but the amiably-disposed Helena, after looking at the undiscriminating youth coldly for a moment, deliberately rose and moved to a vacant spot at a distance. Encouraged by this fragrant act of sympathy I replied with a polite bow to indicate the position, "On the contrary, the story which it is now my presumptuous intention to relate will contain no reference whatever to the carefully-got-up one occupying two empty seats in the front row," and without further introduction began the history of Kao and his three brothers, to which I had added the title, "The Three Gifts."

At the conclusion of this classical example of the snares ever lying around the footsteps of the impious, I perceived that the jocular stripling, whom I had so delicately reproved, was no longer present. Doubtless he had been unable to remain in the same room with the commanding Helena's high-spirited indignation, and anticipating that in consequence there would now be no obstacle to her full-faced benignity, I drew near with an appropriate smile.

It is somewhere officially recorded, "There is only one man who knew with accurate certainty what a maiden's next attitude would be, and he died young of surprise." As I approached I had the sensation of passing into so severe an atmosphere of rigid disfavour, that the ingratiating lines upon my face became frozen in its

99

intensity, despite the ineptness of their expression. Unable to penetrate the cause of my offence, I made a variety of agreeable remarks, until finding that nothing tended towards a becoming reconciliation, I gradually withdrew in despair, and again turned my face in the direction of that same accommodation which I had already found beneath the sign of an Encompassed Goat. Here, by the sarcasm of destiny, I encountered the person who had drawn the slighting analogy between this one's pig-tail and his ability as a story-teller. For a brief space of time the ultimate development of the venture was doubtfully poised, but recognising in each other's features the overhanging cloud of an allied pang, the one before me expressed a becoming contrition for the jest, together with a proffered cup. Not to appear out-classed I replied in a suitable vein, involving the supply of more vessels; whereupon there succeeded many more vessels, called for both singly and in harmonious unison, and the reappearance of numerous bright images, accompanied by a universal scintillation of meteor-like iridescence. In this genial and greatly-enlarged spirit we returned affably together to the hall, and entered unperceived at the moment when the one who made the announcements was crying aloud, "According to the programme the next item should have been a Chinese poem, but as Mr. Kong Ho appears to have left the building, we shall pass him over—"

"What Ho?" exclaimed the somewhat impetuous one by my side, stepping forward indignantly and mounting the platform in his affectionate zeal. "No one shall pass over my old and valued friend—this Ho—while I have a paw to raise. Step forward, Mandarin, and let them behold the inventor and sole user of the justly far-famed G. R. Ko-Ho hair restorer—sent in five guinea bottles to any address on receipt of four penny stamps—as he appeared in his celebrated impersonation of the human-faced Swan at Doll and Edgar's. Come on, oh, Ho!"

"Assuredly," I replied, striving to follow him, "yet with the wary greeting, 'Slowly, slowly; walk slowly,' engraved upon my mind, for the barrier of these convoluted stairs—" but at this word a band of maidens passed out hastily, and in the tumult I reached the dais and began Weng Chi's immortal verses, entitled "The Meandering Flight," which had occupied me three complete days and nights in the detail of rendering the allusions into well-balanced similitudes and at the same time preserving the skilful evasion of all conventional rules which raises the original to so sublime a height.

100

The voice of one singing at the dawn;
The seven harmonious colours in the sky;
The meeting by the fountain;
The exchange of gifts, and the sound of the processional drum;
The emotion of satisfaction in each created being;
This is the all-prominent indication of the Spring.

The general disinclination to engage in laborious tasks;
The general readiness to consume voluminous potions on any
pretext.
The deserted appearance of the city and the absence of the
come-in motion at every door;
The sportiveness of maidens, and even those of maturer age,
ethereally clad, upon the shore.
The avowed willingness of merchants to dispose of their wares
for half the original sum.
This undoubtedly is the Summer.

The yellow tea leaf circling as it falls;
The futile wheeling of the storm-tossed swan;
The note of the marble lute at evening by the pool;
The immobile cypress seen against the sun.
The unnecessarily difficult examination paper.
All these things are suggestive of the Autumn.

The growing attraction of a well-lined couch.
The obsequious demeanour of message-bearers, charioteers,
and
the club-armed keepers of peace.
The explosion of innumerable fire-crackers round the convivial
shines,
The gathering together of relations who at all other times
shun each other markedly.
The obtrusive recollection of a great many things contrary to
a spoken vow, and the inflexible purpose to be more
resolute in future.
These in turn invariably attend each Winter.

It certainly had not presented itself to me before that the words
"invariably attend" are ill-chosen, but as I would have uttered them
their inelegance became plain, and this person made eight
conscientious attempts to soften down their harsh modulation by
various interchanges. He was still persevering hopefully when he of
chief authority approached and requested that the one who was

thus employed and that same other would leave the hall tranquilly, as the all-water entertainment was at an end, and an attending slave was in readiness to extinguish the lanterns.

"Yet," I protested unassumingly, "that which has so far been expressed is only in the semblance of an introductory ode. There follow—"

"You must not argue with the Chair," exclaimed another interposing his voice. "Whatever the Chair rules must be accepted."

"The innuendo is flat-witted," I replied with imperturbable dignity, but still retaining my hold upon the rail. "When this person so far loses his sense of proportion as to contend with an irrational object, devoid of faculties, let the barb be cast. After that introduction dealing with the four seasons, the twelve gong-strokes of the day are reviewed in a like fashion. These in turn give place to the days of the month, then the moons of the year, and finally the years of the cycle."

"That's fair," exclaimed the perverse though well-meaning youth, whom I was beginning to recognise as the cause of some misunderstanding among us. "If you don't want any more of his poem—and I don't blame you—my pal Ho, who is one of the popular Flip-Flap Troupe, offers to do some trick cycle-riding on his ears. What more can you expect?"

"We expect a policeman very soon," replied another severely. "He has already been sent for."

"In that case," said the one who had so persistently claimed me as an ally, "perhaps I can do you a service by directing him here"; and leaving this person to extricate himself by means of a reassuring silence and some of the larger silver pieces of the Island, he vanished hastily.

With some doubt whether or not this deviation into the society of the professedly virtuous, ending as it admittedly does in an involvement, may not be deemed ill-starred; yet hopeful.

KONG HO.

THE THREE GIFTS

*Related by Kong Ho on the occasion of the all-water
disportment, under the circumstances previously set forth.*

BEYOND the limits of the township of Yang-chow there dwelt a rich astrologer named Wei. Reading by his skilful interpretation of the planets that he would shortly Pass Above, he called his sons Chu, Shan, and Hing to his side and distributed his wealth impartially among them. To Chu he gave his house containing a gold couch; to Shan a river with a boat; to Hing a field in which grew a prolific orange-tree. "Thus provided for," he continued, "you will be able to live together in comfort, the resources of each supplying the wants of the others in addition to his own requirements. Therefore when I have departed let it be your first care to sacrifice everything else I leave, so that I also, in the Upper Air, may not be left destitute."

Now in addition to these three sons Wei also had another, the youngest, but one of so docile, respectful, and self-effacing a disposition that he was frequently overlooked to the advantage of his subtle, ambitious, and ingratiating brothers. This youth, Kao, thinking that the occasion certainly called for a momentary relaxation of his usual diffidence, now approached his father modestly, and begged that he also might be included to some trivial degree in his bounty.

This reasonable petition involved Wei in an embarrassing perplexity. Although he had forgotten Kao completely in the division, he had now definitely concluded the arrangement; nor, to his failing powers, did it appear possible to make a just allotment on any other lines. "How can a person profitably cut up an orange-tree, a boat, an inlaid couch, or a house?" he demanded. "Who can divide a flowing river, or what but unending strife can arise from regarding an open field in anything but its entirety? Assuredly six cohesive objects cannot be apportioned between four persons." Yet he could not evade the justice of Kao's implied rebuke, so drawing to his side a jade cabinet he opened it, and from among the contents he selected an ebony staff, a paper umbrella, and a fan inscribed with a mystical sentence. These three objects he placed in Kao's hands, and with his last breath signified that he should use them discreetly as the necessity arose.

When the funeral ceremonies were over, Chu, Shan, and Hing came together, and soon moulded their covetous thoughts into an agreed conspiracy. "Of what avail would be a boat or a river if this person sacrificed the nets and appliances by which the fish are ensnared?" asked Shan. "How little profit would lie in an orange-tree and a field without cattle and the implements of husbandry!" cried Hing. "One cannot occupy a gold couch in an empty house both by day and

103

night," remarked Chu stubbornly. "How inadequate, therefore, would such a provision be for three."

When Kao understood that his three brothers had resolved to act in this outrageous manner he did not hesitate to reproach them; but not being able to contend against him honourably, they met him with ridicule. "Do not attempt to rule us with your wooden staff," they cried contemptuously. "Sacrifice IT if your inside is really sincere. And, in the meanwhile, go and sit under your paper umbrella and wield your inscribed fan, while we attend to our couch, our boat, and our orange-tree."

"Truly," thought Kao to himself when they had departed, "their words were irrationally offensive, but among them there may stand out a pointed edge. Our magnanimous father is now bereft of both comforts and necessities, and although an ebony rod is certainly not much in the circumstances, if this person is really humanely-intentioned he will not withhold it." With this charitable design Kao build a fire before the couch (being desirous, out of his forgiving nature, to associate his eldest brother in the offering), and without hesitation sacrificed the most substantial of his three possessions.

It here becomes necessary to explain that in addition to being an expert astrologer, Wei was a far-seeing magician. The rod of unimpressionable solidity was in reality a charm against decay, and its hidden virtues being thus destroyed, a contrary state of things naturally arose, so that the next morning it was found that during the night the gold couch had crumbled away into a worthless dust.

Even this manifestation did not move the three brothers, although the geniality of Shan and Hing's countenances froze somewhat towards Chu. Nevertheless Chu still possessed a house, and by pointing out that they could live as luxuriantly as before on the resources of the river and the field and the tree, he succeeded in maintaining his position among them.

After seven days Kao reflected again. "This avaricious person still has two objects, both of which he owes to his revered father's imperishable influence," he admitted conscience-stricken, "while the being in question has only one." Without delay he took the paper umbrella and ceremoniously burned it, scattering the ashes this time upon Shan's river. Like the rod the umbrella also possessed secret virtues, its particular excellence being a curse against clouds, wind demons, thunderbolts and the like, so that during the night a great storm raged, and by the morning Shan's boat had been washed away.

This new calamity found the three brothers more obstinately perverse than ever. It cannot be denied that Hing would have withdrawn from the guilty confederacy, but they were as two to one, and prevailed, pointing out that the house still afforded shelter, the river yielded some of the simpler and inferior fish which could be captured from the banks, and the fruitfulness of the orange-tree was undiminished.

At the end of seven more days Kao became afflicted with doubt. "There is no such thing as a fixed proportion or a set reckoning between a dutiful son and an embarrassed sire," he confessed penitently. "How incredibly profane has been this person's behaviour in not seeing the obligation in its unswerving necessity before." With this scrupulous resolve Kao took his last possession, and carrying it into the field he consumed it with fire beneath Hing's orange-tree. The fan, in turn, also had hidden properties, its written sentence being a spell against drought, hot winds, and the demons which suck the nourishment from all crops. In consequence of the act these forces were called into action, and before another day Hing's tree had withered away.

It is said with reason, "During the earthquake men speak the truth." At this last disaster the impious fortitude of the three brothers suddenly gave way, and cheerfully admitting their mistake, each committed suicide, Chu disembowelling himself among the ashes of his couch, Shan sinking beneath the waters of his river, and Hing hanging by a rope among the branches of his own effete orange-tree.

When they had thus fittingly atoned for their faults the imprecation was lifted from off their possessions. The couch was restored by magic art to its former condition, the boat was returned by a justice-loving person into whose hands it had fallen lower down the river, and the orange-tree put out new branches. Kao therefore passed into an undiminished inheritance. He married three wives, to commemorate the number of his brothers, and had three sons, whom he called Chu, Shan, and Hing, for a like purpose. These three all attained to high office in the State, and by their enlightened morals succeeded in wiping all the discreditable references to others bearing the same names from off the domestic tablets.

From this story it will be seen that by acting virtuously, yet with an observing discretion, on all occasions, it is generally possible not only to rise to an assured position, but at the same time unsuspectedly to involve those who stand in our way in a just destruction.

LETTER XIII

*Concerning a state of necessity; the arisings engendered
thereby, and the turned-away face of those ruling the
literary quarter of the city towards one possessing a style.
This foreign manner of feigning representations, and
concerning my dignified portrayal of two.*

VENERATED SIRE,—It is now more than three thousand years ago
that the sublime moralist Tcheng How, on being condemned by a
resentful official to a lengthy imprisonment in a very inadequate oil
jar, imperturbably replied, "As the snail fits his impliant shell, so
can the wise adapt themselves to any necessity," and at once coiled
himself up in the restricted space with unsuspected agility. In times
of adversity this incomparable reply has often shone as a steadfast
lantern before my feet, but recently it struck my senses with a
heavier force, for upon presenting myself on the last occasion at the
place of exchange frequented by those who hitherto have carried out
your spoken promise with obliging exactitude, and at certain stated
intervals freely granted to this person a sufficiency of pieces of gold,
merely requiring in return an inscribed and signet-bearing record of
the fact, I was received with no diminution of sympathetic urbanity,
indeed, but with hands quite devoid of outstretched fulness.

In a small inner chamber, to which I was led upon uttering
courteous protests, one of solitary authority explained how the
deficiency had arisen, but owing to the skill with which he entwined
the most intricate terms in unbroken fluency, the only impression
left upon my superficial mind was, that the person before me was
imputing the scheme for my despoilment less to any mercenary
instinct on the part of his confederates, than to a want of timely
precision maintained by one who seemed to bear an agreeable-
sounding name somewhat similar to your own, and who, from the
difficulty of reaching his immediate ear, might be regarded as
dwelling in a distant land. Encouraged by this conciliatory
profession (and seeing no likelihood of gaining my end otherwise), I
thereupon declared my willingness that the difference lying between
us should be submitted to the pronouncement of dispassionate
omens, either passing birds, flat and round sticks, the seeds of two

107

oranges, wood and fire, water poured out upon the ground or any equally reliable sign as he himself might decide. However, in spite of his honourable assurances, he was doubtless more deeply implicated in the adventure than he would admit, for at this scrupulous proposal the benignant mask of his expression receded abruptly, and, striking a hidden bell, he waved his hands and stood up to signify that further justice was denied me.

In this manner a state of destitution calling for the fullest acceptance of Tcheng How's impassive philosophy was created, nor had many hours faded before the first insidious temptation to depart from his uncompromising acquiescence presented itself.

At that time there was no one in whom I reposed a larger-sized piece of confidence (in no way involving sums of money,) than one officially styled William Beveledge Greyson, although, profiting by our own custom, it is unusual for those really intimate with his society to address him fully, unless the occasion should be one of marked ceremony. Forming a resolution, I now approached this obliging person, and revealing to him the cause of the emergency, I prayed that he would advise me, as one abandoned on a strange Island, by what handicraft or exercise of skill I might the readiest secure for the time a frugal competence.

"Why, look here, aged man," at once replied the lavish William Greyson, "don't worry yourself about that. I can easily let you have a few pounds to tide you over. You will probably hear from the bank in the course of a few days or weeks, and it's hardly worth while doing anything eccentric in the meantime."

At this delicately-worded proposal I was about to shake hands with myself in agreement, when the memory of Tcheng How's resolute submission again possessed me, and seeing that this would be an unworthy betrayal of destiny I turned aside the action, and replying evasively that the world was too small to hold himself and another equally magnanimous, I again sought his advice.

"Now what silly upside-down idea is it that you've got into that Chinese puzzle you call your head, Kong?" he replied; for this same William was one who habitually gilded unpalatable truths into the semblance of a flattering jest. "Whenever you turn off what you are saying into a willow-pattern compliment and bow seventeen times like an animated mandarin, I know that you are keeping something back. Be a man and a brother, and out with it," and he struck me heavily upon the left shoulder, which among the barbarians is a

108

proof of cordiality to be esteemed much above the mere wagging of each other's hands.

"In the matter of guidance," I replied, "this person is ready to sit unreservedly on your well-polished feet. But touching the borrowing of money, obligations to restore with an added sum after a certain period, initial-bearing papers of doubtful import, and the like, I have read too deeply the pointed records of your own printed sheets not to prefer an existence devoted to the scraping together of dust at the street corners, rather than a momentary affluence which in the end would betray me into the tiger-like voracity of a native money-lender."

"Well, you do me proud, Kong," said William Beveledge, after regarding me fixedly for a moment. "If I didn't remember that you are a flat-faced, slant-eyed, top-side-under, pig-tailed old heathen, I should be really annoyed at your unwarrantable personalities. Do you take ME for what you call a 'native money-lender'?"

"The pronouncements of destiny are written in iron," I replied inoffensively, "and it is as truly said that one fated to end his life in a cave cannot live for ever on the top of a pagoda. Undoubtedly as one born and residing here you are native, and as inexorably it succeeds that if you lend me pieces of gold you become a money-lender. Therefore, though honourably inspired at the first, you would equally be drawn into the entanglement of circumstance, and the unevadible end must inevitably be that against which your printed papers consistently warn one."

"And what is that?" asked Beveledge Greyson, still regarding me closely, as though I were a creature of another part.

"At first," I replied, "there would be an alluring snare of graceful words, tea, and the consuming of paper-rolled herbs, and the matter would be lightly spoken of as capable of an easy adjustment; which, indeed, it cannot be denied, is how the detail stands at present. The next position would be that this person, finding himself unable to gather together the equivalent of return within the stated time, would greet you with a very supple neck and pray for a further extension, which would be permitted on the understanding that in the event of failure his garments and personal charms should be held in bondage. To escape so humiliating a necessity, as the time drew near I would address myself to another, one calling himself William, perchance, and dwelling in a northern province, to whom I would be compelled to assign my peach-orchard at Yuen-ping. Then by varying degrees of infamy I would in turn be driven to visit a certain Bevel of the Middle Lands, a person Edge carrying on his insatiable traffic on the southern coast, one Grey elsewhere, and a Mr. Son, of the west, who might make an honourable profession of lending money without any security whatever, but who in the end would possess himself of my ancestral tablets, wives, and inlaid coffin, and probably also obtain a lien upon my services and prosperity in the Upper Air. Then, when I had parted from all comfort in this life, and every hope of affluence in the Beyond, it would presently be disclosed that all these were in reality as one person who had unceasingly plotted to my destruction, and William Beveledge Greyson would stand revealed in the guise of a malevolent vampire. Truly that development has at this moment an appearance of unreality, and worthy even of pooh-pooh, but thus is the warning spread by your own printed papers and the records of your Halls of Justice, and it would be an unseemly presumption for one of my immature experience to ignore the outstretched and warning finger of authority."

"Well, Kong," he said at length, after considering my words attentively, "I always thought that your mental outlook was a hash of Black Art, paper lanterns, blank verse, twilight, and delirium tremens, but hang me if you aren't sound on finance, and I only wish that you'd get some of my friends to look at the matter of borrowing in your own reasonable, broad-minded light. The question is, what next?"

I replied that I leaned heavily against his sagacious insight, adding, however, that even among a nation of barbarians one who could repeat the three hundred and eleven poems comprising the Book of Odes from beginning to end, and claim the degree "Assured Genius" would ever be certain of a place.

"Yes," replied William Greyson,—"in the workhouse. Put your degree in your inside pocket, Kong, and don't mention it. You'll have far more chance as a distressed mariner. The casual wards are full of B.A.'s, but the navy can't get enough A.B.'s at any price. What do you say to an organ, by the way? Mysterious musicians generally go down well, and I dare say there's room for a change from veiled ladies, persecuted captains and indigent earls. You ought to make a sensation."

"Is it in the nature of melodious sounds upon winding a handle?" I asked, not at the moment grasping with certainty to what organ he referred.

"Well, some call them that," he admitted, "others don't. I suppose, now, you wouldn't care to walk to Brighton with your feet tied together, or your hair in curl papers, and then get on at a music hall? Or would there be any chance of your Legation kidnapping you if it was properly worked? 'Kong Ho, the great Chinese Reformer, tells the Story of his Life,'—there ought to be money in it. Are you a reformer or the leader of a secret society, Kong?"

"On the contrary," I replied, "we of our Line have ever been unflinching in our loyalty to the dynasty of Tsing."

"You ought to have known better, then. It's a poor business being that in your country nowadays. Pity there are no bye-elections on the African Labour Question, or you'd be snapped up for a procession."

To this I replied that although the idea of moving in a processional triumph would readily ensnare the minds of the light and fantastic, I should prefer some more literary occupation, submissively adding that in such a case I would not stiffen my joints against the most menial lot, even that of blending my voice in a laudatory chorus, or of carrying official pronouncements about the walls of the city, for it is said with justice, "The starving man does not peel his melon, nor do the parched first wipe round the edges of the proffered cup."

"If you've set your mind on something literary," said Beveledge confidently, "you have every chance of finishing up in a chorus or carrying printed placards about the streets, certainly. When it comes to that, look me up in Eastcheap." With this encouraging assurance of my ultimate success he left me, and rejoicing that I had not fallen into the snare of opposing a written destiny, I sought the literary quarters of the city.

When this person has been able to write of any custom or facet of existence here in a strain of conscientious esteem, he has not hesitated to dip his brush deeply into the inkpot. Reverting backwards, this barbarian enactment of not permitting those who from any cause have decided upon spending the night in a philosophical abstraction to repose upon the public seats about the swards and open spaces is not conceived in a mood of affable toleration. Nevertheless there are deserted places beyond the furthest limits of the city where a more amiable full-face is shown. On the eleventh day of this one's determination to sustain himself by the exercise of his literary style, he was journeying about sunset towards one of these spots, subduing the grosser instincts of

111

mankind by reviewing the wisdom of the sublime Lao Ch'un, who decided that heat and cold, pain and fatigue, and mental distress, have no real existence, and are therefore amenable to logical disproof, while the cravings of hunger and thirst are merely the superfluous attributes of a former and lower state of existence, when a passer-by, who for some distance had been alternately advancing before and remaining behind, matched his footsteps into mine.

"Whichee way walk-go, John, eh?" said this unfortunate being, who appeared to be suffering from a laborious deformity of speech. "Allee samee load me. Chin-chin."

Filled with compassion for one who evidently found himself alone in a strange land, in the absence of his more highly-accomplished companion, unable to indicate his wants and requirements to those about him, I regretfully admitted that I had not chanced to encounter that John whose wandering footsteps he sought; and to indicate, by not leaving him abruptly, that I maintained a sympathetic concern over his welfare, I pointed out to him the exceptional brilliance of the approaching night, adding that I myself was then directing a course towards a certain spacious Heath, a few li distant in the north.

"Sing-dance tomollow, then?" he said, with a condensed air of general disappointment. "Chop-chop in a pay look-see show on Ham—Hamstl—oh damme! on 'Ampstead 'Eath? Booked up, eh, John?"

Gradually convinced that it was becoming necessary to readjust the significance of the incident, I replied that I had no intention of partaking of chops or food of any variety in an erected tent, but merely of passing the night in an intellectual seclusion.

"Oh," said the one who was walking by my side, regarding my garments with engaging attention, and at the same time appearing to regain an unruffled speech as though the other had been an assumed device, "I understand—the Blue Sky Hotel. Well, I've stayed there once or twice myself. A bit down on your uppers, eh?"

"Assuredly this person may perchance lay his upper parts down for a short space of time," I admitted, when I had traced out the symbolism of the words. "As it is humanely written in The Books, 'Sleep and suicide are the free refuges equally of the innocent and the guilty.'"

112

"Oh, come now, don't," exclaimed the energetic person, striking himself together by means of his two hands. "It's sinful to talk about suicide the day before bank holiday. Why, my only Somali warrior has vamoosed with his full make-up, and the Magnetic Girl too, and I never thought of suicide—only whether to turn my old woman into a Veiled Beauty of the Harem or a Hairy Lama from Tibet."

Not absolutely grasping the emergency, yet in a spirit of inoffensive cordiality I remarked that the alternative was insufferably perplexing, while he continued.

"Then I spotted you, and in a flash I got an idea that ought to take and turn out really great if you'll come in. Now follow this: Missionary's tent in the wilds of Pekin. Domestic interior by lamp-light. Missionary (me) reading evening paper; missionary's wife (the missus) making tea, and between times singing to keep the small pet goat quiet (small goat, a pillow, horsecloth, and pocket-handkerchief). Breaks down singing, sobs, and says she feels a strange all-over presentiment. Missionary admits being a bit fluffed himself, and lets out about a notice signed in blood that he's seen in the city."

"Carried upon a pole?" this person demanded, feeling that something of a literary nature might yet be wrested into the incident.

"On a flagstaff if you like," conceded the other one magnanimously. "A notice to the effect that it is the duty of every jack mother's son of them to douse the foreign devils, man, woman, and child, and especially the talk-book pass-hat-round men. Also that he has had several brick-ends heaved at him on his way back. Then stops suddenly, hits his upper crust, and says that it's like his blamed fat-headedness to frighten her; while she clutches at herself three times and faints away."

"Amid the voluminous burning of blue lights?" suggested this person resourcefully.

"By rights there should be," admitted the one who was devising the representation; "but it will hardly run to it. Anyway, it costs nothing to turn the lamp down—saves a bit in fact, and gives an effect. Then outside, in the distance at first you understand, you begin to work up the sound of the advancing mob—rattles, shouts, tum-tums, groans, tin plates and all that one mortal man can do with hands, feet and mouth."

"With the interspersal of an occasional cracker and the stirring notes produced by striking a hollow wooden fish repeatedly?" I cried; for let it be confessed that amid the portrayal of the scene my imagination had taken an allotted part.

"If you like to provide them, and don't set the bally show on fire," he replied. "Anyhow, these two aren't supposed to notice anything even when the row gets louder. Then it drops and you are heard outside talking in whispers to the others—words of command and telling them to keep back half-a-mo, and so on. See?"

"Doubtless introducing a spoken charm and repeating the words of an incantation against omens, treachery, and other matters."

"Next a flap of the tent down on the floor is raised, and you reconnoitre, looking your very worst and holding a knife between your teeth and another in each hand. Wave a hand to your followers to keep back—or come on: it makes no difference. Then you crawl in on your stomach, give a terrific howl, and stab me in the back. That rolls me under the curtain, and so lets me out. The missus ups with the wood-chopper and stands before the cradle, while you yell and dance round with the knives. That ought to be made 'the moment' of the whole piece. The great thing is to make enough noise. If you can yell louder than the talking-machine outfit on the next pitch we ought to turn money away. While you are at it I start a fresh row outside—shouts, cheers, groans, words of command and a paper bag or two. Seeing that the game is up you make a rush at the old woman; she downs you with the chopper, turns the lamp up full, shakes out a Union Jack over the sleeping infant, and finally stands in her finest attitude with one hand pointing impressively upwards and the other contemptuously downwards just as Rule Britannia is played on the cornet outside and I appear at the door in a general's full uniform and let down the curtain."

For acting in the manner designated—as touching the noises both inside and out, the set dance with upraised knives, the casting to earth of himself, and being myself in turn vanquished by the aged female, with an added compact that from time to time I should be led by a chain and shown to the people from a raised platform—we agreed upon a daily reward of two pieces of silver, an adequacy of food, and a certain ambiguously-referred-to share of the gain. It need not be denied that with so favourable an opportunity of introducing passages from the Classics a much less sum would have been accepted, but having obtained this without a struggle, the one now recounting the facts raised the opportune suggestion of an inscribed placard, in order to fulfil the portent foreshadowed by William Greyson.

"Oh, we'll star you, never fear," assented the accommodating personage, and having by this time reached that spot upon the Heath where his Domestic Altar had been raised, we entered.

"All the most distinguished actors in this country take another name," he said reflectively, when he had drawn forth a parchment of praiseworthy dimensions and ink of three colours, "and though I have nothing to say against Kong Ho Tsin Cheng Quank Paik T'chun Li Yuen Nung for quiet unostentatious dignity, it doesn't have just the grip and shudder that we want. Now how does 'Fang' strike you?" and upon my courteous acquiescence that this indeed united within it those qualities which he required, he traced its characters in red ink upon a lavish scale.

"'Fang Hung Sin' about fits the idea of snap and bloodthirstiness, I should say," he continued, and using the brush and all the colours with an expert proficiency which would infallibly gain him an early recognition at any of our competitive examinations, he presently laid before me the following gracefully-composed notice, which was suspended from a conspicuous pole about the door of the tent on the following day.

> FANG HUNG SIN
> The Captured Boxer Chieftain.
>
> Under a strong guard, and by arrangement with the British and
> Chinese authorities concerned,
>
> Fang Hung Sin
>
> Will positively re-enact the GORY SCENES of CARNAGE in which
> he took a LEADING and SANGUINARY PART during the LATE RISING.
>
> ALONE IN PEKIN
> Or, What a Woman can do.
>
> PANEL I. PEACE: The Missionary's Tent by Night—All's Well—
> The Dread Warning—"I am by your side, Beloved."

PANEL II. ALARM: The Signal—The Spy—The Mob Outside—
Treachery—"Save Yourself, my Darling"—"And Leave
You? Never!"

PANEL III. REVENGE: The Attack—The Blow Falls—Who Can
Save
Her Now?—"Back, Renegade Viper!"—The English Guns
—"Rule Britannia!"

FANG HUNG SIN, The Desperado.
There is only one FANG, and he must be seen.
FANG! FANG!! FANG!!!

I will not upon this occasion, esteemed one, delay myself with an account of this barbarian Festival of Lanterns; or, as their language would convey it, Feast of Cocoa-nuts, beyond admitting that with the possible exception of an important provincial capital during the triennial examinations I doubt whether our own unapproachable Empire could show a more impressively-extended gathering, either in the diverse and ornamental efflorescence of head garb, in the affectionate display openly lavished by persons of one sex towards those of the other, or even one more successful in our own pre-eminent art of producing the multitudinous harmony of conflicting sounds.

At the appointed hour this person submitted himself to be heavily shackled, and being led out before the assembled crowd, endeavoured by a smiling benignity of manner and by reassuring signs of welcome, to produce a favourable impression upon their sympathies and to allure them within. This pacific face was undoubtedly successful, however offensively the ill-conditioned one who stood by was inspired to express himself behind his teeth, for the space of the tent was very quickly occupied and the actions of simulation were to begin.

Without doubt it might have been better if this person had first made himself more fully acquainted with the barbarian manner of acting. The fact that this imagined play, which even in one of our inferior theatres would have filled the time pleasantly for two or three months, was to be compressed into the narrow limits of seven minutes and a half, should reasonably have warned him that amid the ensuing rapidity of word and action, most of the leisurely courtesies and all the subtle range of concealed emotion which embellish our own wood pavement must be ignored. But it is well and suggestively written, "The person who deliberates sufficiently before taking every step will spend his life standing upon one leg." In the past this one had not found himself to be grossly inadequate on any arising emergency, and he now drew aside the hanging drapery and prepared to carry out a preconcerted part with intrepid self-reliance.

It has already been expressed, that the reason and incentive urging me to a ready agreement lay in the opportunities by which suitable passages from the high Classics could be discreetly woven into the fabric of the plot, and the occupation thereby permeated with an honourable literary flavour. In accordance with this resolve I blended together many imperishable sayings of the wisest philosophers to present the cries and turmoil of the approaching mob, but it was not until I protruded my head beneath the hanging canopy in the guise of one observing that an opportunity arose of a really well-sustained effort. In this position I recited Yung Ki's stimulating address to his troops when in sight of an overwhelming foe, and, in spite of the continually back-thrust foot of the undiscriminating one before me, I successfully accomplished the seventy-five lines of the poem without a stumble. Then entering fully, with many deprecatory bows and expressions of self-abasement at taking part in so seemingly detestable an action, I treacherously, yet with inoffensive tact, struck the one wearing an all-round collar delicately upon the back. Not recognising the movement, or being in some other way obtuse, the person in question instead of sinking to the ground turned hastily to me in the form of an inquiry, leaving me no other reasonable course than to display the knife openly to him, and to assure him that the fatal blow had already been inflicted. Undoubtedly his immoderate retorts were inept at such a moment, nor was his ensuing strategy of turning completely round three times, striking himself about the head and body, and uttering ceremonious curses before he fell devoid of life—as though the earlier remarks had been part of the ordained scheme—to any degree convincing, and the cries of disapproval from the onlookers proved that they also regarded this one as the victim of an unworthy rebuke.

"Not if the benches were filled at half a guinea a head would I take on another performance like that," exclaimed the one with whom I was associated, when it was over. "Besides the dead loss of lasting three quarters of an hour it's tempting providence when the seats are movable. I suppose it isn't your fault, Kong, you poor creature, but you haven't got no glare and glitter. There's only one thing for it:

you must be the Rev. Mr. Walker and I'll take Fang." He then robed himself in my attire, guided me among the intricacies of the all-round collar and outer garments in exchange, hung a slender rope about his back, and after completing the artifice by a skilful device of massing coloured inks upon our faces, he commanded me to lead him out by a chain and observe intelligently how a captive Boxer chief should disport himself.

No sooner had we reached the platform than the one whom I controlled leapt high into the air, dragged me to the edge of the erection, showed his teeth towards the assembly and waved his arms menacingly at them; then turning upon this person, he inflamed his face with passion, rattled his chain furiously, and uttered such vengeance-laden cries that, unable to subdue the emotion of fear, I abandoned all pretence, and dropping the chain, fled to the furthest recess of the tent, followed by the still threatening Fang.

There is an expression among us, "Cheng-hu was too considerate: he tried to drive nails with a cucumber." Cheng-hu would certainly have quickly found the necessity of a weapon of three-times hardened steel if he had lived among these barbarians, who are insensible to the higher forms of politeness, in addition to acting in a contrary and illogical manner on all occasions. Instead of being repelled and discouraged by Fang's outrageous behaviour, they clamoured to be admitted into the tent more vehemently than before, and so successfully established the venture that the one to whom I must now allude throughout as Fang signified to me his covetous intention of reducing the performance by a further two and a half minutes in order to reap an added profit and to garner all his rice before the Hoang Ho rose.

As for myself, revered, it would be immature to hold the gauze screen of prevarication between your all-discerning mind and my own trepidation. From the moment when I first saw the expression of utterly depraved malignity and deep-seared hate which he had cunningly engraved upon his face by means of the coloured inks, I was far from being comfortably settled within myself. Even the society of the not inelegant being of the inner chamber, whom it was now my part to console with alluring words and movements, could not for some time retain my face from a back-way instinct at every sound; but when the detail was reached that she sank into my grasp bereft of all energy, and for the first time I was just succeeding in forgetting the unpropitious surroundings, the one Fang, who had

118

entered with unseemly stealth, suddenly hurled his soul-freezing battle-cry upon my ear and leapt forward with uplifted knife. Perceiving the action from an angle of my eye even as he propelled himself through the air, I could not restrain an ignoble wail of despair, and not scrupling to forsake the maiden, I would have taken refuge beneath a couch had he not seized my outer robe and hurled me to the ground. From this point to the close of the entertainment the vigorous person in question did not cease from raising cries and challenges in an unfaltering and many-fathomed stream, while at the same time he continued to spring from one extremity of the stage to the other surrounded by every external attribute of an insatiable tiger-like rage. It is circumstantially related that the one near at hand, who has been referred to as possessing a voiced machine, became demented, and bearing the contrivance to a certain tent erected by the charitable, entreated them to remove the impediment from its speech so that it might be heard again and his livelihood restored. When the action of brandishing a profusion of knives before the lesser one's eyes was reached, so nerve-shattering was the impression which Fang created that the back of the tent had to be removed in order to let out those who no longer had possession of themselves, and to let in those—to a ten-fold degree—who strove for admission on the rumour spreading that something exceptionally repellent was progressing within.

With what attenuated organs of repose this person would have reached the end of so strenuous an occupation had he been compelled to twelve enactments each hour throughout the gong-strokes of the day without any literary relief, it is not enticing to dwell upon. This evil was averted by a timely intervention, for upon proceeding to the outer air for the third time I at once perceived among the foremost throng the engaging full-face of William Beveledge Greyson. This really painstaking individual had learned, as he afterwards explained, that the chiefs of exchange (those who in the first case had opposed me resolutely,) had received a written omen, and now in contrition were expressing their willingness to hold out a full restitution. With this assurance he had set forth in an unremitting search, and guided by street-watchers, removers of superfluous earth, families propelling themselves forward upon one foot, astrologers, two-wheeled charioteers, and others who move early and secretly by night, he had traced my description to this same Heath. Here he had been attracted by the displayed placard (remembering my honourable boast), and approaching nearer, he had plainly recognised my voice within. But in spite of this the successful disentanglement was by no means yet accomplished.

Not expecting so involved a reversal of things, and being short-eyed by nature, William Greyson did not wait for a fuller assurance than to be satisfied that the one before him wore my robes and conformed in a general outline, before he addressed him.

"Kong Ho," he said pleasantly, "what the Chief Evil Spirit are you doing up there?" adding persuasively, "Come down, there's a good fellow. I have something important to tell you."

Thus appealed to, the one Fang hesitated in doubt, seeing on the one hand a certain loss of face if he declined the conversation, and on the other hand having no clear perception of what was required from him. Therefore he entered upon a course of evasion and somewhat incapably replied, "Chow Chop Wei Hai Wei Lung Tung Togo Kuroki Jim Jam Beri Beri."

"Don't act the horned sheep," said Beveledge, who was both resolute and one easily set into violent motion by an opposing stream. "Come down, or I'll come up and fetch you." And not being satisfied with Fang's ill-advised attempt to express himself equivocally, those around took up the apt similitude of a self-opinionated animal, and began to suggest a comparison to other creatures no less degraded.

"Rats yourselves!" exclaimed the easily-inflamed person at my side, losing the inefficient cords of his prudence beneath the sting. "Who's a rabbit? For two guinea-pigs I'd mow all the grass between here and the Spaniards with your own left ears," and not permitting me sufficient preparation to withhold the chain more firmly, he abruptly cast himself down among them, amid a scene of the most untamed confusion.

"Oh, affectionately-disposed brethren," I exclaimed, moving forward and raising my hand in refined disapproval, "the sublime Confucius, in the twenty-third chapter of the book called 'The Great Learning,' warns us against—" but before I could formulate the allusion Beveledge Greyson, who at the sound of my conciliatory words had gazed first in astonishment and then in a self-convulsed position, drew himself up to my side, and taking a firm grasp upon the all-round collar, projected me without a pause through the tent, and only halting for a moment to point significantly back to the varied and animated scene behind, where, amid a very profuse display of contending passions, the erected stage was already being dragged to the ground, and a band of the official watch was in the act of converging from every side, he led me through more deserted paths to the scene of a final extrication.

With a well-gratified sense of having held an unswerving course along the convoluted outline of Destiny's decree, to whatever tending.

KONG HO.

LETTER XIV

Concerning a pressing invitation from an ever benevolently-disposed father to a prosaic but dutifully-inclined son. The recording of certain matters of no particular moment. Concerning that ultimate end which is symbolic of the inexorable wheels of a larger Destiny.

VENERATED SIRE,—It is not for the earthworm to say when and in what exact position the iron-shod boot shall descend, and this person, being an even inferior creature for the purpose of the comparison, bows an acquiescent neck to your very explicit command that he shall return to Yuen-ping without delay. He cannot put away from his mind a clinging suspicion that this arising is the result of some imperfection in his deplorable style of correspondence, whereby you have formed an impression quite opposed to that which it had been the intention to convey, and that, perchance, you even have a secret doubt whether upon some specified occasion he may not have conducted the enterprise to an ignoble, or at least not markedly successful, end. However, the saying runs, "The stone-cutter always has the last word," and you equally, by intimating with your usual unanswerable and clear-sighted gift of logic that no further allowance of taels will be sent for this one's dispersal, diplomatically impose upon an ever-yearning son the most feverish anxiety once more to behold your large and open-handed face.

Standing thus poised, as it may be said, for a returning flight across the elements of separation, it is not inopportune for this person to let himself dwell gracefully upon those lighter points of recollection which have engraved themselves from time to time upon his mind without leading to any more substantial adventure worthy to record. Many of the things which seemed strange and incomprehensible when he first came among this powerful though admittedly barbarian people, are now revealed at a proper angle; others, to which he formerly imagined he had found the disclosing key, are, on the other hand, plunged into a distorting haze; while between these lie a multitude of details in every possible stage of disentanglement and doubt. As a final and painstaking pronouncement, this person

122

has no hesitation in declaring that this country is not—as practically all our former travellers have declared—completely down-side-up as compared with our own manners and customs, but at the same time it is very materially sideways.

Thus, instead of white, black robes are the indication of mourning; but as, for the generality, the same colour is also used for occasions of commerce, ceremony, religion, and the ordinary affairs of life, the matter remains exactly as it was before. Yet with obtuse inconsistency the garments usually white—in which a change would be really noticeable—remain white throughout the most poignant grief. How much more markedly expressed would be the symbolism if during such a period they wore white outer robes and black body garments. Nevertheless it cannot be said that they are unmindful of the emblematic influence of colour, for, unlike the reasonable conviction that red is red and blue is blue, which has satisfied our great nation from the days of the legendary Shun, these pale-eyed foreigners have diverged into countless trifling imaginings, so that when the one who is now expressing his contempt for the development required a robe of a certain hue, he had to bend his mouth, before he could be exactly understood, to the degrading necessity of asking for "Drowned-rat brown," "Sunstroke magenta," "Billingsgate purple," "London milk azure," "Settling-day green," or the like. In the other signs of mourning they do not come within measurable distance of our pure and uncomfortable standard. "If you are really sincere in your regret for the one who has Passed Beyond, why do you not sit upon the floor for seven days and nights, take up all food with your fingers, and allow your nails to grow untrimmed for three years?" was a question which I at first instinctively put to lesser ones in their affliction. In every case save one I received answers of evasive purport, and even the one stated reason, "Because although I am a poor widder I ain't a pig," I deemed shallow.

I have already dipped a revealing brush into the subject of names. Were the practice of applying names in a wrong and illogical sequence maintained throughout it might indeed raise a dignified smile, but it would not appear contemptible; but what can be urged when upon an occasion one name appears first, upon another occasion last? A dignity is conferred in old age, and it is placed before the family designation borne by an honoured father and a direct line of seventeen revered ancestors. Another title is bestowed, and eats up the former like a revengeful dragon. New distinctions follow, some at one end, others at another, until a very successful person may be suitably compared to the ringed oleander snake, which has the power of growing equally from either the head or the tail. To express the matter by a definite allusion, how much more graceful and orchideous, even in a condensed fashion, would appear the designation of this selected one, if instead of the usual form of the country it was habitually set forth in the following logical and thoroughly Chinese style:—Chamberlain Joseph, Master, Mr., Thrice Wearer of the Robes and Golden Collar, One of the Just Peacemakers, Esquire, Member of the House of Law-givers, Leader in the Council of Commerce, Presider over the Tables of Provincial Government, Uprightly Honourable Secretary of the Outlying Parts.

Among the notes which at various times I have inscribed in a book for future guidance I find it written on an early page, "They do not hesitate to express their fathers' names openly," but to this assertion there stands a warning sign which was added after the following incident. "Is it true, Mr. Kong," asked a lesser one, who is spoken of as vastly rich but discontented with her previous lot, of this person upon an occasion, "is it really true that your countrymen to not consider it right to speak of their fathers' names, even in this enlightened age?" To this I replied that the matter was as she had eloquently expressed it, and, encouraged by her amiable condescension, I asked after the memory of her paternal grandsire, whose name I had frequently heard whispered in connection with her own. To my inelegant confusion she regarded me for a period as though I had the virtue of having become transparent, and then passed on in a most overwhelming excess of disconcertingly-arranged silence.

"You've done it now, Kong," said one who stood by (or, as we would express the same thought, "You have succeeded in accomplishing the undesirable"); "don't you know that the old man was in the tripe and trotter line?"

"To no degree," I replied truly. "Yet," I continued, matching his idiom with another equally facile, "wherein was this person's screw loose? Are they not openly referred to—those of the Line of Tripe and Trotter—by their descendants?"

"Not in most cases," he said, with a concentration that indicated a lurking sting among his words. "Generally speaking, they aren't mentioned or taken into any account whatever. While they are alive they are kept in the background and invited to treat themselves to the Tower when nice people are expected; when dead they are fastened up in the family back cupboard by a score of ten-inch nails and three-trick Yale locks, so to speak. And in the meantime all the splash is being made on their muddy oof. See?"

I nodded agreeably, though, had the opportunity been more favourable, I would have made the feint to learn somewhat more of this secret practice of burying in the enclosed space beneath the stairs. Thus is it set forth why, after the statement, "They do not hesitate to express their fathers' names openly," it is further written, "Walk slowly! Engrave well upon your discreet remembrance the unmentionable Line of Tripe and Trotter."

Another point of comparison which the superficial have failed to record is to be found in the frequent encouragements to regard The Virtues which are to be seen, like our own Confucian extracts, freely inscribed on every wall and suitable place about the city. These for the most part counsel moderation in taking false oaths, in stepping heedlessly upon the unknown ground, in following paths which lead to doubtful ends, and other timely warnings. "Beware a smoke-breathing demon," is frequently cast across one's path upon a barrier, and this person has never failed to accept the omen and to retrace his steps hastily without looking to the right or the left. Even our own national caution is not forgotten, although to conform to barbarian indolence it is written, "Slowly, slowly; drive slowly." "Keep to the Right" (or, "Abandon that which is evil," as the analogy holds,) is perhaps the most frequently displayed of all, and doubtless many charitable persons obtain an ever-accruing merit by hanging the sign bearing these words upon every available post. Others are of a stern and threatening nature, designed to make the most hardened ill-doer pause, as—in their own tongue—"Rubbish may be shot here"; which we should render, "At any moment, and in such a place as this, a just doom and extinction may overtake the worthless." This inscription is never to be seen except in waste expanses, where it points its significance with a multiplied force. There is another definite threat which is lavishly set out, and so thoroughly that it may be encountered in the least frequented and almost inaccessible spots. This, as it may be translated, reads, "Trespass not the forbidden. The profligate may flourish like the gourd for a season, but in the end assuredly they will be detected, and justice meted out with the relentless fury of the written law."

In a converse position, the wide difference in the ceremonial forms of retaliatory invective has practically disarmed this usually eloquent person, and he long since abandoned every hope of expressing himself with any satisfaction in encounters of however acrimonious a trend. At first, with an urbane smile and gestures of dignified contempt, he impugned the authenticity of the Ancestral Tablets of those with whom he strove, in an unbroken stream of most bitter contumely. Finding them silent under this reproach, he next lightly traced their origin back through generations of afflicted lepers, deformed ape-beings, and Nameless Things, to a race of primitive ghouls, and then went on in relentless fluency to predict an early return in their descendants to the condition of a similar state. For some time he had a well-gratified assurance that those whom he assailed were so overwhelmed as to be incapable of retort, and in this belief he never failed to call upon passers-by to witness his triumph; but on the fourth occasion a young man whom I had thus publicly denounced for a sufficient though forgotten reason, after listening courteously to my venomous accusations, bestowed a two-cash piece upon me and passed on, remarking that it was hard, and those around, also, would have added from their stores had it been permitted. From this time onward I did not attempt to make myself disagreeable either in public or to those whom I esteemed privately. On the other hand, the barbarian manner of retort did not find me endowed by nature to parry it successfully. Quite lacking in measured periods, it aims, by an extreme rapidity of thrust and an insincerity of sequence, to entangle the one who is assailed in a complication of arising doubts and emotions. "Who are you,—no one but yourself," exclaimed a hireling of hung-dog expression who claimed to have exchanged pledging gifts with a certain maiden who stood, as it were, between us, and falling into the snare, I protested warmly against the insult, and strove to disprove the inference before the paralogism lay revealed. Throughout the whole range of the Odes, the Histories, the Analects, and the Rites what recognised formula of rejoinder is there to the taunt, "Oh, go and put your feet in mustard and cress"; or how can one, however skilled in the highest Classics, parry the subtle inconsistencies of the reproach, "You're a nice bit of orl right, aren't you? Not arf, I don't think."

Among the arts of this country that of painting upon canvas is held in repute, but to a person associated with the masterpieces of the Ma epoch these native attempts would be gravity-dispelling if they were not too reminiscent of the torture chamber. It is rarely, indeed, that even the most highly-esteemed picture-makers succeed in depicting every portion of a human body submitted to their brush, and not infrequently half of the face is left out. Once, when asked by a paint-applier who was entitled to append two signs of exceptional distinction behind his name, to express an opinion upon a finished work, I diffidently called his attention to the fact that he had forgotten to introduce a certain exalted one's left ear. "Not at all, Mr. Kong," he replied, with an expression of ill-merited self-satisfaction, "but it is hidden by the face." "Yet it exists," I contended; "why not, therefore, press it to the front at all hazard, rather than send so great a statesman down into the annals of posterity as deformed to that extent?" "It certainly exists," he admitted, "and one takes that for granted; but in my picture it cannot be seen." I bowed complaisantly, content to let so damaging an admission point its own despair. A moment later I continued, "In the great Circular Hall of the Palace of Envoys there is a picture of two camels, foot-tethered, as it fortunately chanced, to iron rings. Formerly there were a drove of eight—the others being free—so exquisitely outlined in all their parts that one night, when the door had been left incautiously open, they stepped down from the wall and escaped to the woods. How deplorable would have been the plight of these unfortunate beings, if upon passing into the state of a living existence they had found that as a result of the limited vision of their creator they only possessed twelve legs and three whole bodies among them."

Perchance this tactfully-related story, so applicable to his own deficiencies, may sink into the imagination of the one for whom it was inoffensively unfolded. Yet doubt remains. Our own picture-judgers take up a position at the side of work when they with to examine its qualities, retiring to an ever-diminishing angle in order to bring out the more delicate effects, until a very expert and conscientious critic will not infrequently stand really behind the picture he is considering before he delivers a final pronouncement. Not until these native artists are able to regard their crude attempts from the other side of the canvas can they hope to become equally proficient. To this fatal shortcoming must be added that of insatiable ambition, which prompts the young to the portrayal of widely differing subjects. Into the picture-room of one who might thus be described this person was recently conducted, to pass an opinion upon a scene in which were depicted seven men of varying nationalities and appropriately garbed, one of the opposing sex carrying a lighted torch, an elephant reclining beneath a fruitful vine, and the President of a Republic. For a period this person resisted the efforts of those who would have questioned him, withdrawing their attention to the harmonious lights upon the river mist floating far below, but presently, being definitely called upon, he replied as follows: "Mih Ying, who was perhaps the greatest of his time, spent his whole life in painting green and yellow beetles in the act of concealing themselves beneath dead maple leaves upon the approach of day. At the age of seventy-five he burst into tears, and upon being approached for a cause he exclaimed, 'Alas, if only this person had resisted the temptation to be diffuse, and had confined himself to green beetles alone, he might now, instead of contemplating a misspent career, have been really great.' How much less," I continued, "can a person of immature moustaches hope to depict two such conflicting objects as a recumbent elephant and the President of a Republic standing beneath a banner?"

Upon the temptation to deal critically with the religious instincts of the islanders this person draws an obliterating brush. As practically every traveller who has honoured our unattractive land with his effusive presence has subsequently left it in a printed record that our ceremonies are grotesque, our priesthood ignorant and depraved, our monasteries and sacred places spots of plague upon an otherwise flower-adorned landscape, and our beliefs and sacrifices only worthy to exist for the purpose of being made into jest-origins by more refined communities, the omission on this one's part may appear uncivil and perhaps even intentionally discourteous. To this, as a burner of joss-sticks and an irregular person, he can only reply by a deprecatory waving of both hands and a reassuring smile.

With the two-sided memories of many other details hanging thickly around his brush, it would not be an achievement to continue to a practically inexhaustible amount. As of the set days when certain things are observed, among which fall the first of the fourth month (but that would disclose another involvement), another when flat cakes are partaken of without due caution, another when rounder cakes are even more incautiously consumed, and that most brightly-illuminated of all when it is permissible to embrace maidens openly, and if discreetly accomplished with no overhanging fear of ensuing forms of law, beneath the emblem of a suspended branch, in memory of the wisdom of certain venerable sages who were doubtless expert in the practice. As of the inconvenient custom when two persons are walking together that they should arrange themselves side by side, to the obvious discomfort of others, the sweeping away of all opportunities for agreeable politeness, and the utter disregard of the time-honoured example of the sagacious water-fowl. As of the inconsistency of refusing, even with contempt, to receive our most intimate form of regard and use this person's lip-cloth after a feast, yet the mulish eagerness in that same youth to drink from a cup previously used by a lesser one. As of the precision (which still remains a cloud of doubt,) with which creatures so intractable as the bull are successfully trained to roar aloud at certain gong-strokes of the day as an agreed signal. As of the streets in movement, the lights at evening, and the voices of those unseen. As of these and as of other matters, so multitudinous that they crowd about this person's mind like the assembling swallows, circling above the deserted millet fields before they turn their beaks to the sea, and dropping his brush (perchance with an acquiescent sigh), he, also, kow-tows submissively to a blind but appointed destiny, and prepares to seek a passage from an alien land of sojourning.

With the impetuous craving of an affectionate son to behold a revered sire, intensified by the fact that he has reached the innermost lining of his sleeve; with affectionate greetings towards Ning, Hia-Fa, and T'ian Yen, and an assurance that they have never been really absent from his thoughts.

KONG HO.

Ernest Bramah, of whom in his lifetime Who's Who had so little to say, was born in Manchester. At seventeen he chose farming as a profession, but after three years of losing money gave it up to go into journalism. He started as correspondent on a typical provincial paper, then went to London as secretary to Jerome K. Jerome, and worked himself into the editorial side of Jerome's magazine, To-day, where he got the opportunity of meeting the most important literary figures of the day. But he soon left To-day to join a new publishing firm, as editor of a publication called The Minister; finally, after two years of this, he turned to writing as his full-time occupation. He was intensely interested in coins and published a book on the English regal copper coinage. He is, however, best known as the creator of the charming character Kai Lung who appears in Kai Lung Unrolls His Mat, Kai Lung's Golden Hours, The Wallet of Kai Lung, Kai Lung Beneath the Mulberry Tree, The Mirror of Kong Ho, and The Moon of Much Gladness; he also wrote two one-act plays which are often performed at London variety theatres, and many stories and articles in leading periodicals. He died in 1942.